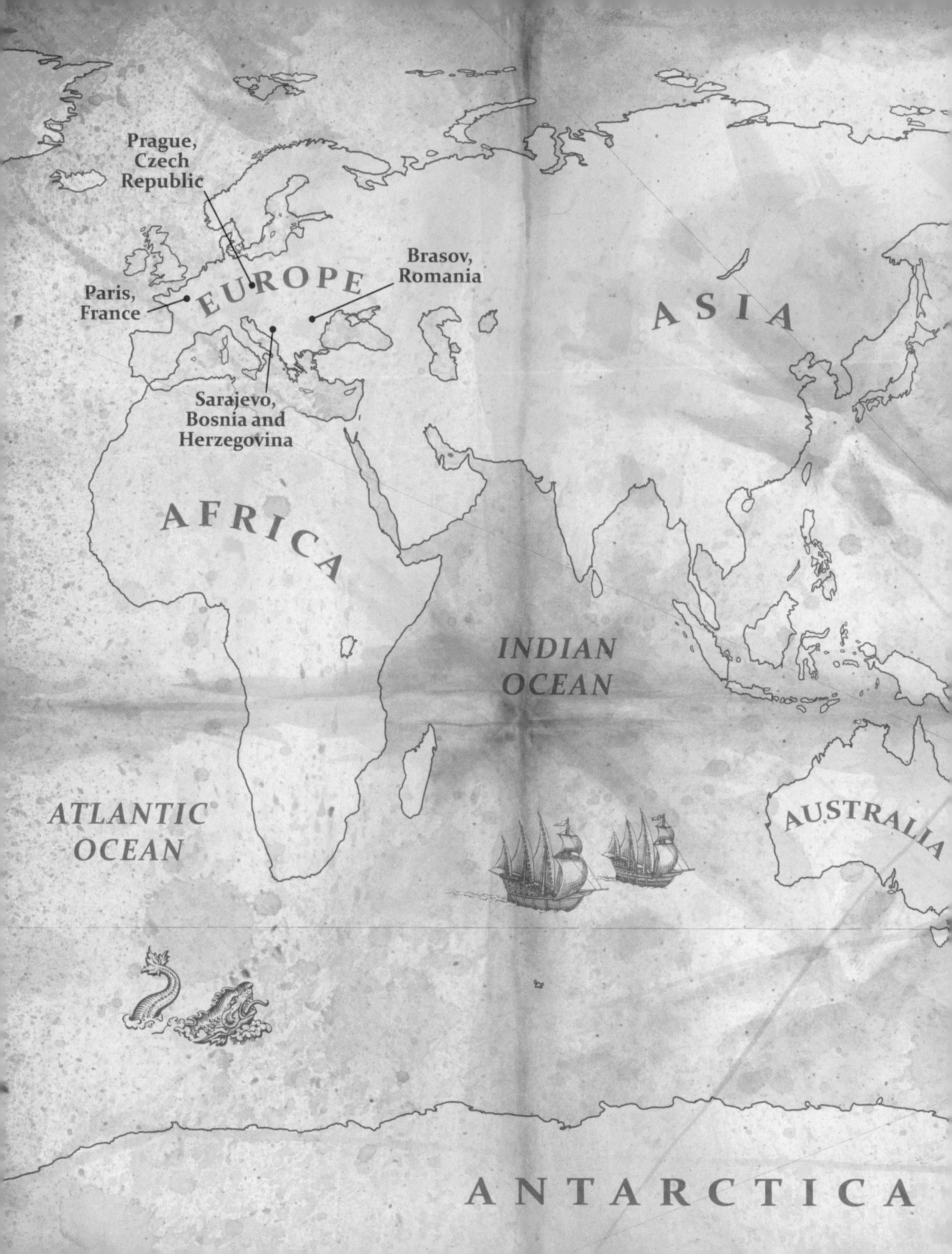
Prague, Czech Republic
Paris, France
EUROPE
Brasov, Romania
ASIA
Sarajevo, Bosnia and Herzegovina
AFRICA
INDIAN OCEAN
ATLANTIC OCEAN
AUSTRALIA
ANTARCTICA

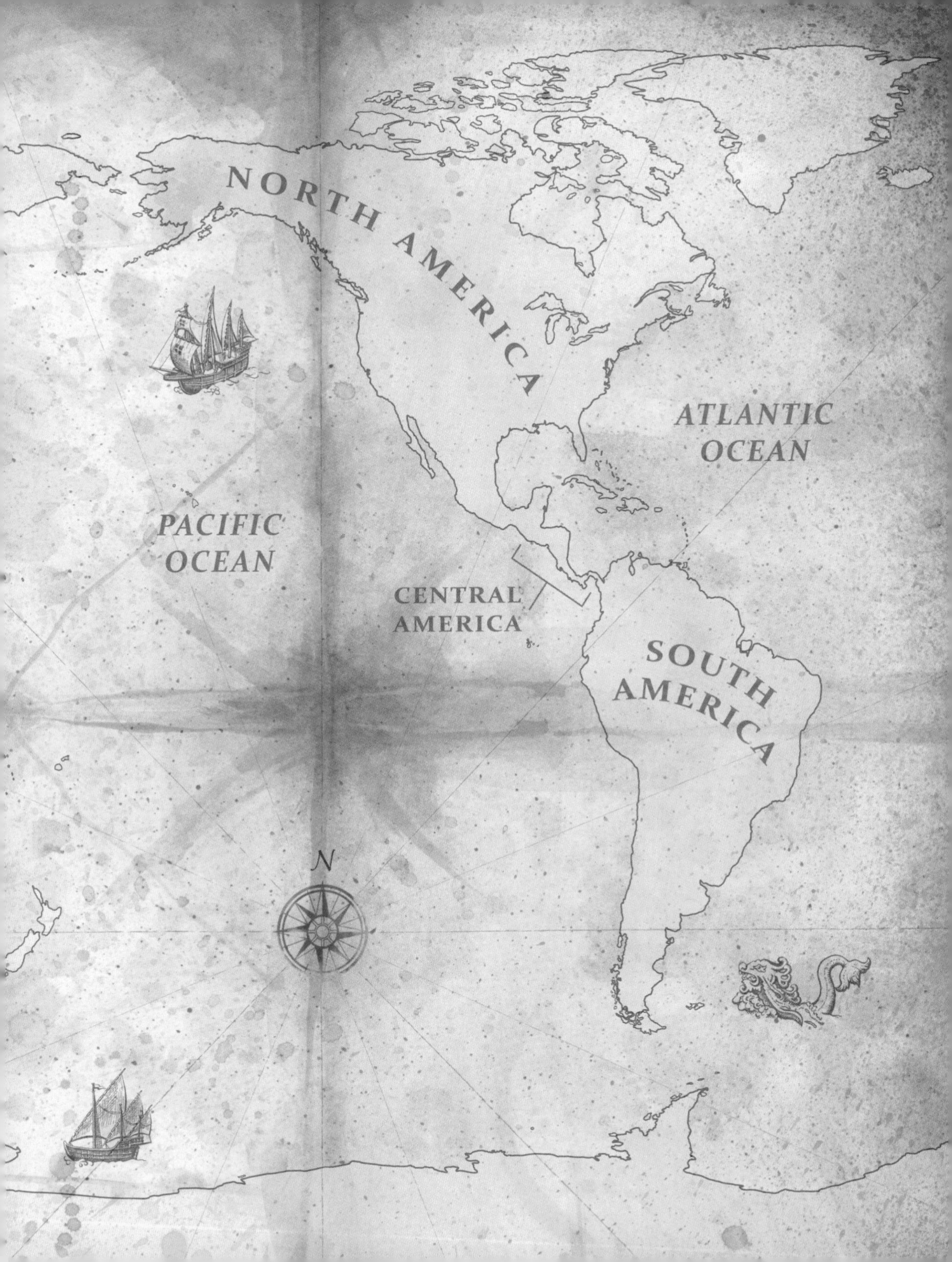
NORTH AMERICA
ATLANTIC OCEAN
PACIFIC OCEAN
CENTRAL AMERICA
SOUTH AMERICA
N

THE SECRET MUMMY

LARS JAKOBSEN

GRAPHIC UNIVERSE™ • MINNEAPOLIS • NEW YORK

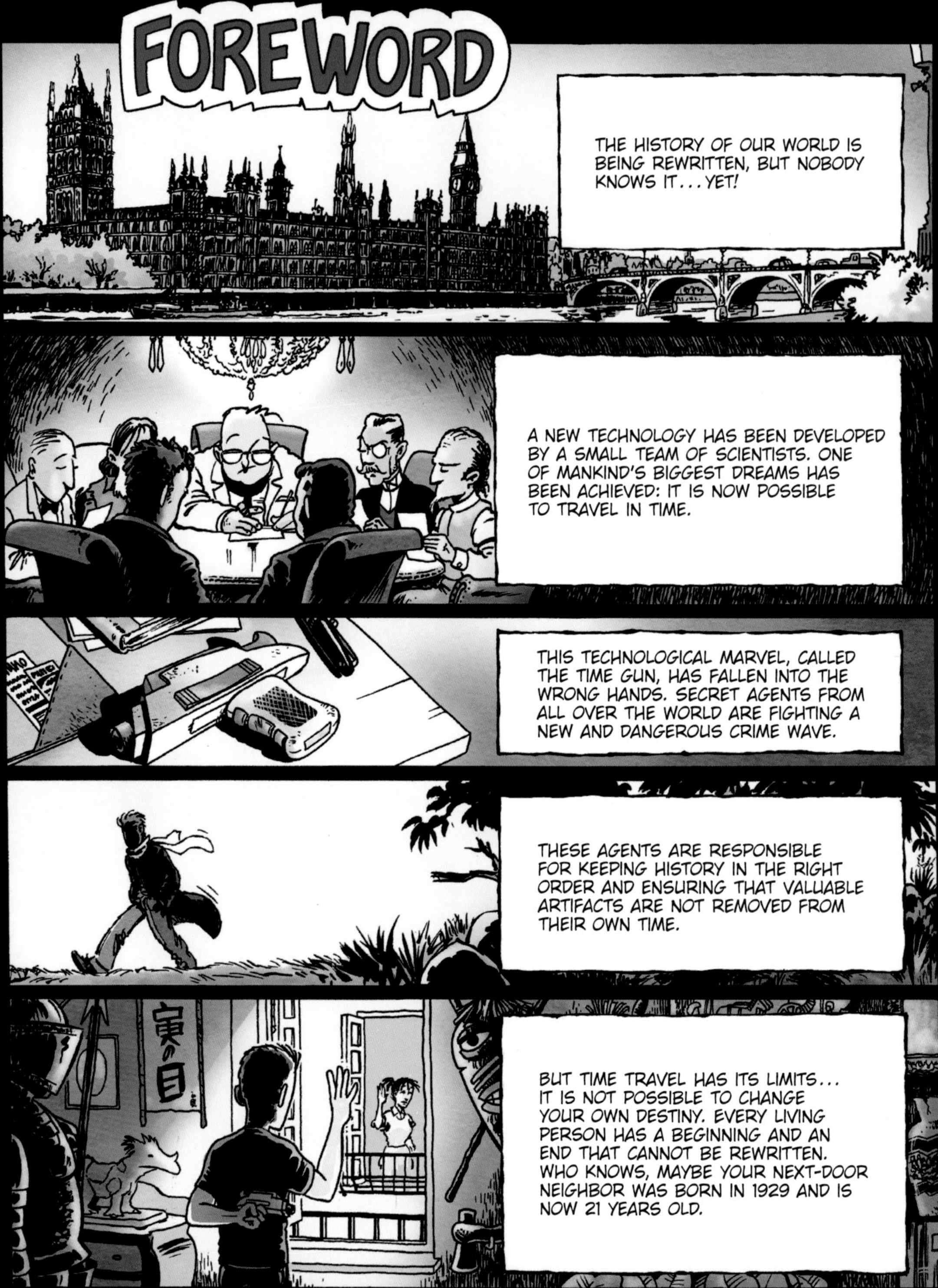
FOREWORD
THE HISTORY OF OUR WORLD IS BEING REWRITTEN, BUT NOBODY KNOWS IT... YET!
A NEW TECHNOLOGY HAS BEEN DEVELOPED BY A SMALL TEAM OF SCIENTISTS. ONE OF MANKIND'S BIGGEST DREAMS HAS BEEN ACHIEVED: IT IS NOW POSSIBLE TO TRAVEL IN TIME.
THIS TECHNOLOGICAL MARVEL, CALLED THE TIME GUN, HAS FALLEN INTO THE WRONG HANDS. SECRET AGENTS FROM ALL OVER THE WORLD ARE FIGHTING A NEW AND DANGEROUS CRIME WAVE.
THESE AGENTS ARE RESPONSIBLE FOR KEEPING HISTORY IN THE RIGHT ORDER AND ENSURING THAT VALUABLE ARTIFACTS ARE NOT REMOVED FROM THEIR OWN TIME.
BUT TIME TRAVEL HAS ITS LIMITS... IT IS NOT POSSIBLE TO CHANGE YOUR OWN DESTINY. EVERY LIVING PERSON HAS A BEGINNING AND AN END THAT CANNOT BE REWRITTEN. WHO KNOWS, MAYBE YOUR NEXT-DOOR NEIGHBOR WAS BORN IN 1929 AND IS NOW 21 YEARS OLD.

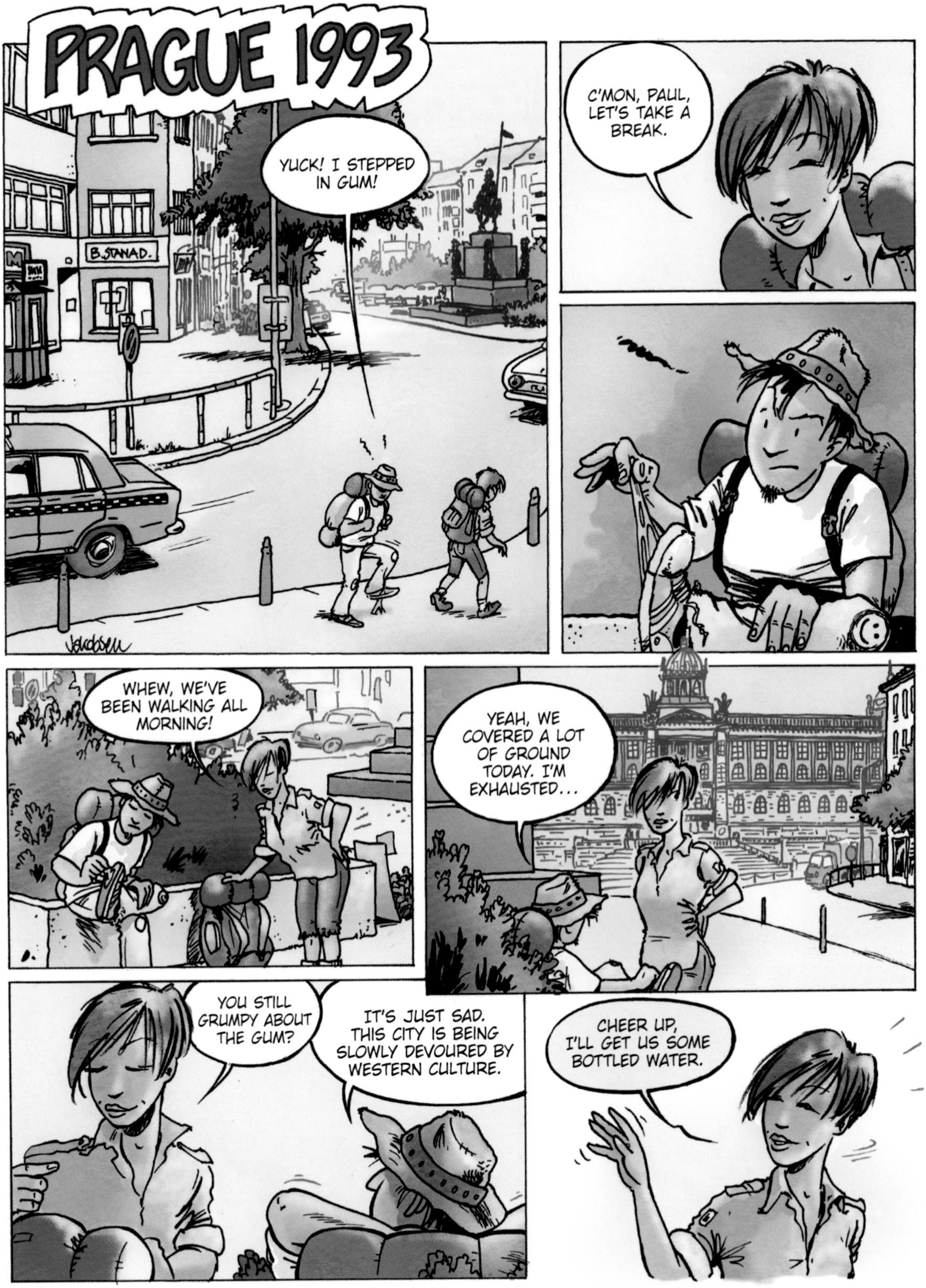
PRAGUE 1993
B. STANAD.
YUCK! I STEPPED IN GUM!
C'MON, PAUL, LET'S TAKE A BREAK.
WHEW, WE'VE BEEN WALKING ALL MORNING!
YEAH, WE COVERED A LOT OF GROUND TODAY. I'M EXHAUSTED...
YOU STILL GRUMPY ABOUT THE GUM?
IT'S JUST SAD. THIS CITY IS BEING SLOWLY DEVOURED BY WESTERN CULTURE.
CHEER UP, I'LL GET US SOME BOTTLED WATER.

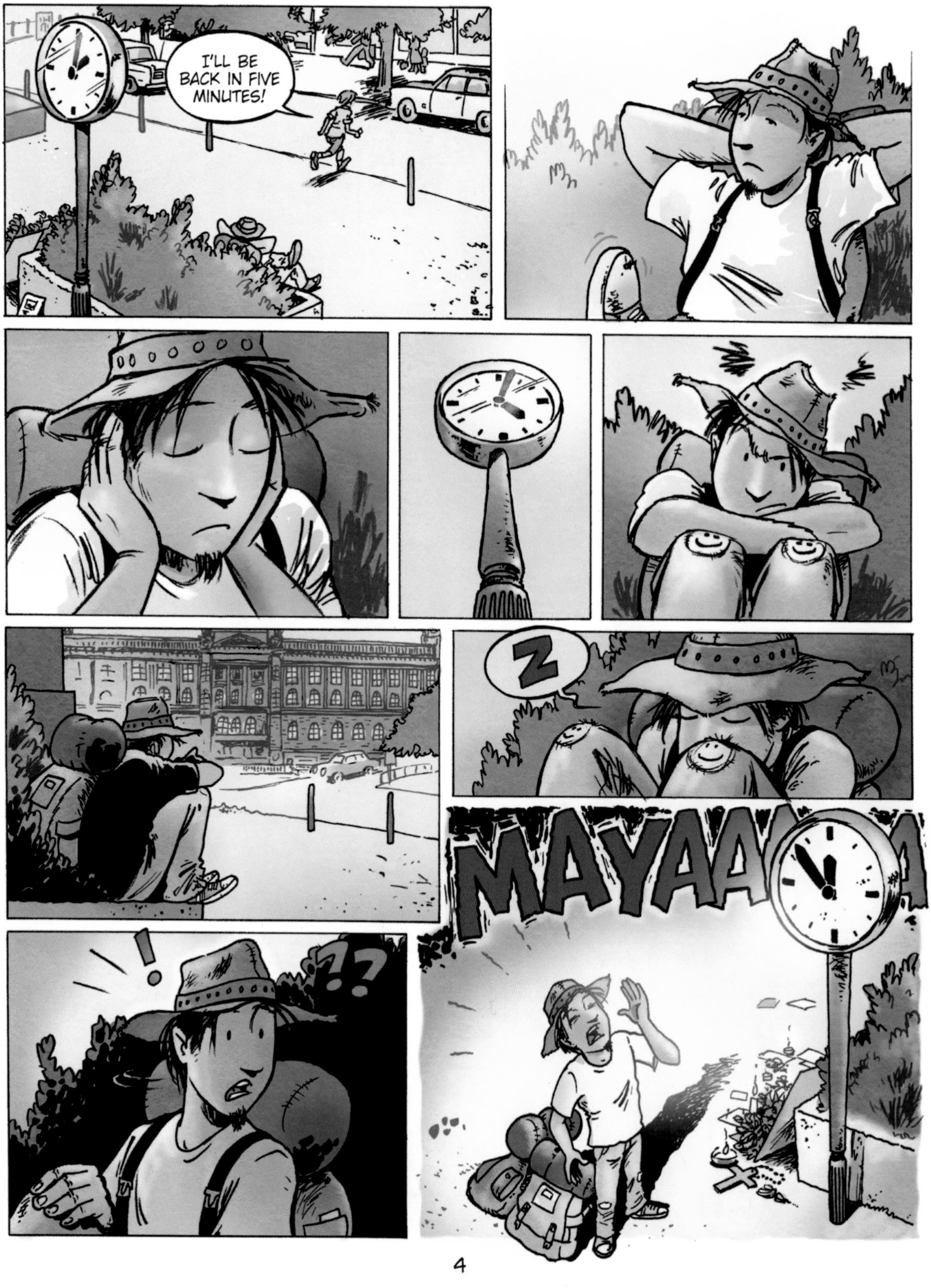
I'LL BE BACK IN FIVE MINUTES!
Z
MAYAAA
!
??

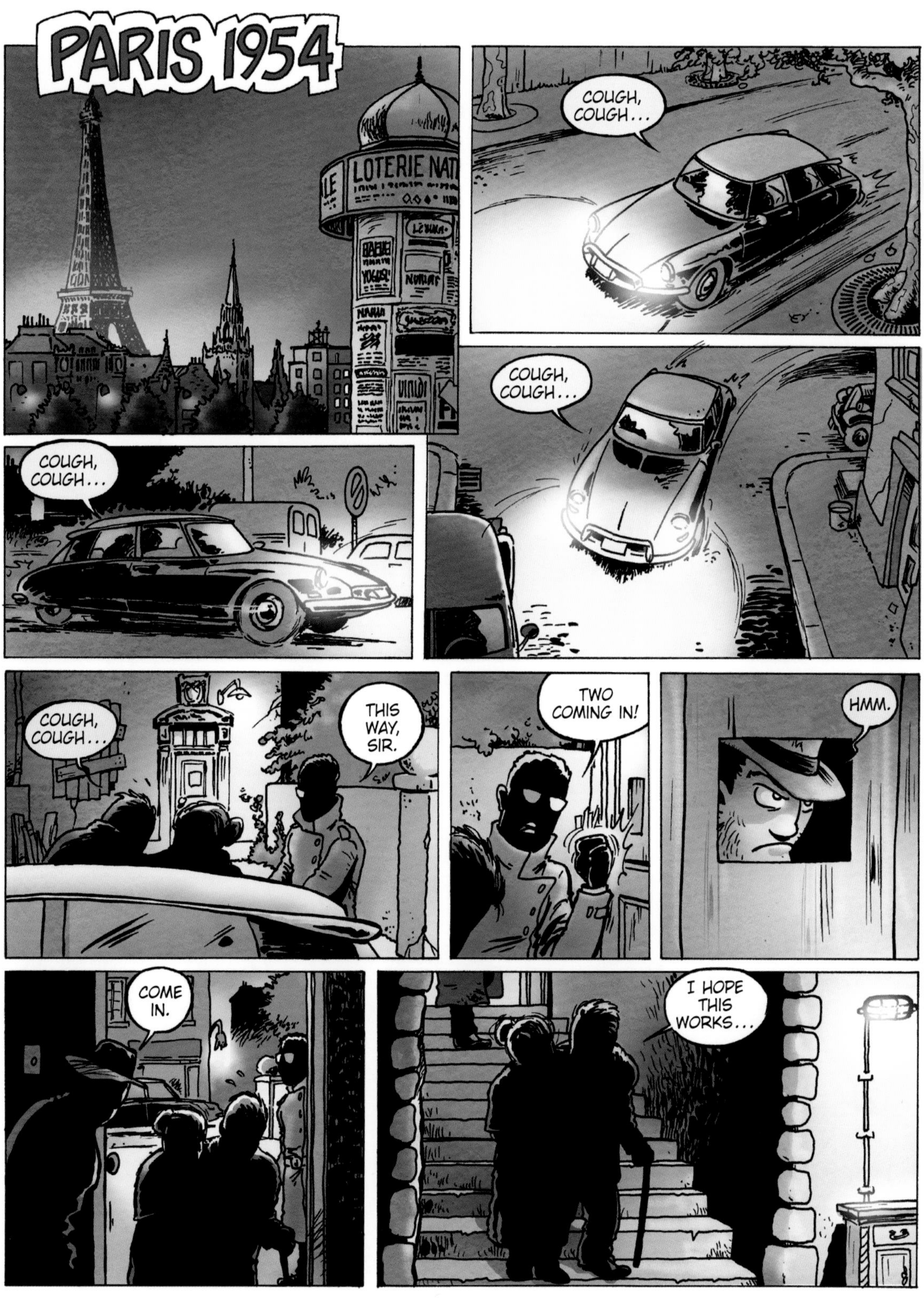
PARIS 1954
LOTERIE NAT
COUGH, COUGH...
COUGH, COUGH...
COUGH, COUGH...
COUGH, COUGH...
THIS WAY, SIR.
TWO COMING IN!
HMM.
COME IN.
I HOPE THIS WORKS...

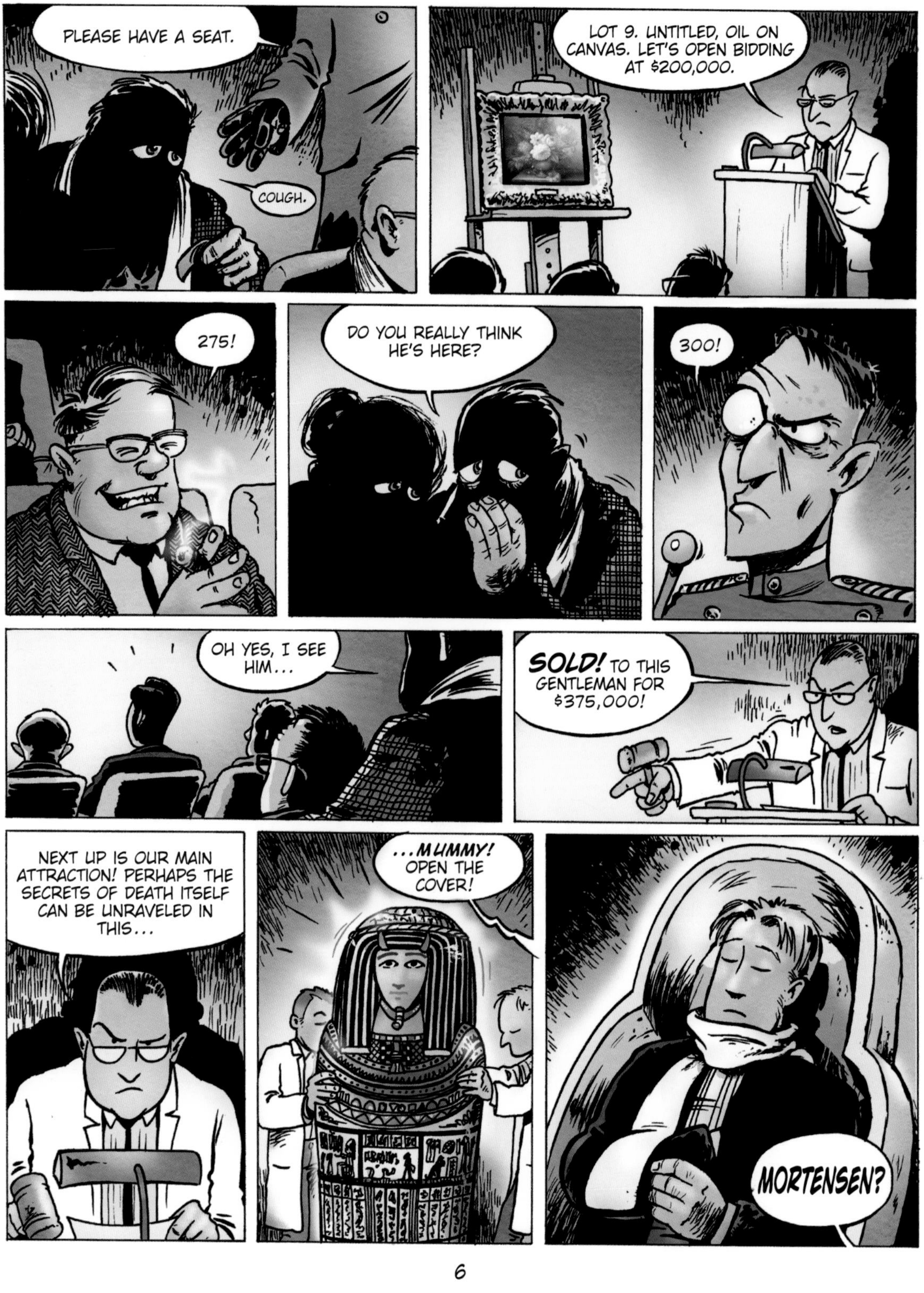
PLEASE HAVE A SEAT.
COUGH.
LOT 9. UNTITLED, OIL ON CANVAS. LET'S OPEN BIDDING AT $200,000.
275!
DO YOU REALLY THINK HE'S HERE?
300!
OH YES, I SEE HIM...
SOLD! TO THIS GENTLEMAN FOR $375,000!
NEXT UP IS OUR MAIN ATTRACTION! PERHAPS THE SECRETS OF DEATH ITSELF CAN BE UNRAVELED IN THIS...
...MUMMY! OPEN THE COVER!
MORTENSEN?

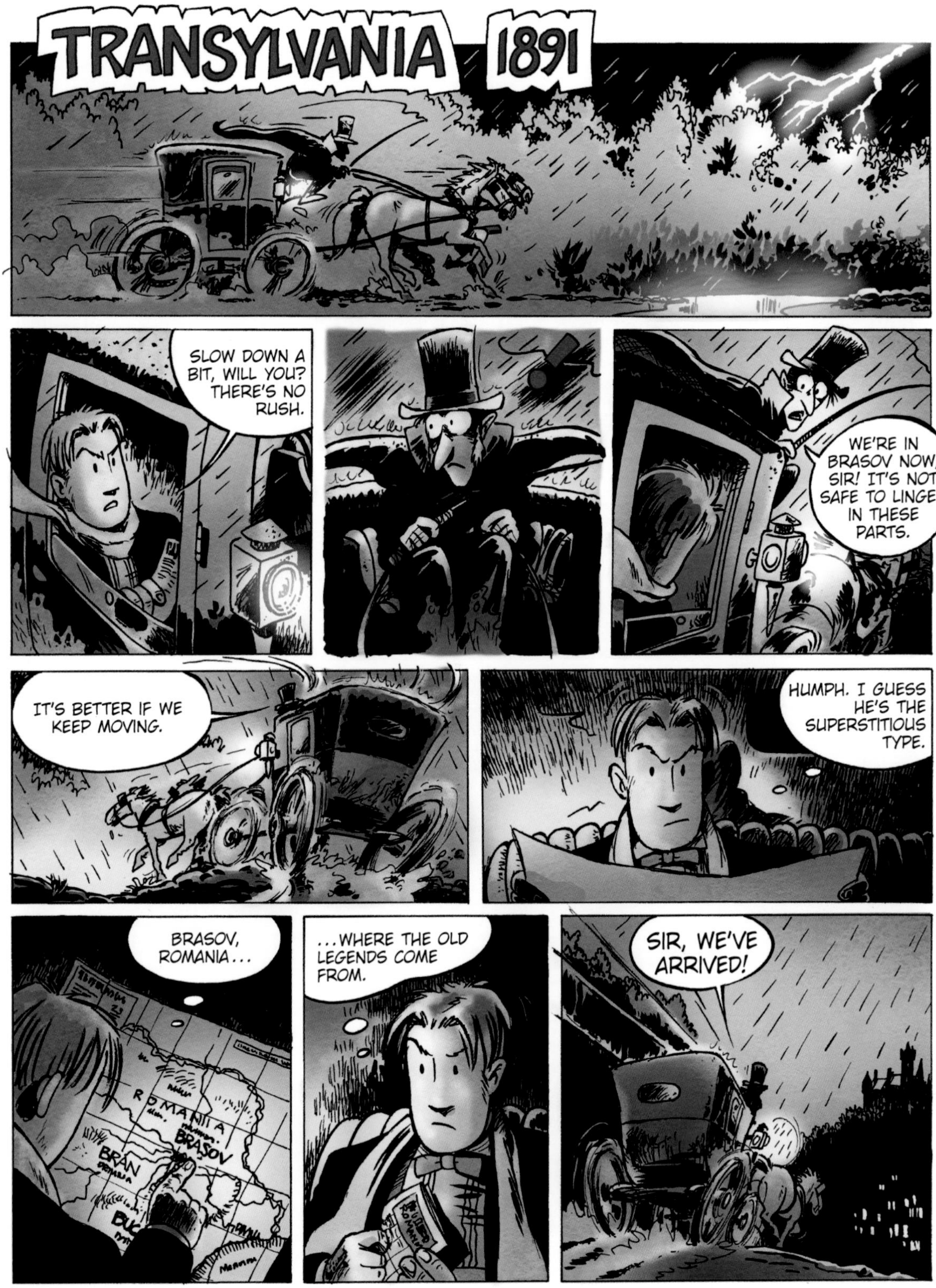
TRANSYLVANIA 1891
SLOW DOWN A BIT, WILL YOU? THERE'S NO RUSH.
WE'RE IN BRASOV NOW, SIR! IT'S NOT SAFE TO LINGER IN THESE PARTS.
IT'S BETTER IF WE KEEP MOVING.
HUMPH. I GUESS HE'S THE SUPERSTITIOUS TYPE.
BRASOV, ROMANIA...
ROMANIA
BRASOV
BRAN
...WHERE THE OLD LEGENDS COME FROM.
SIR, WE'VE ARRIVED!

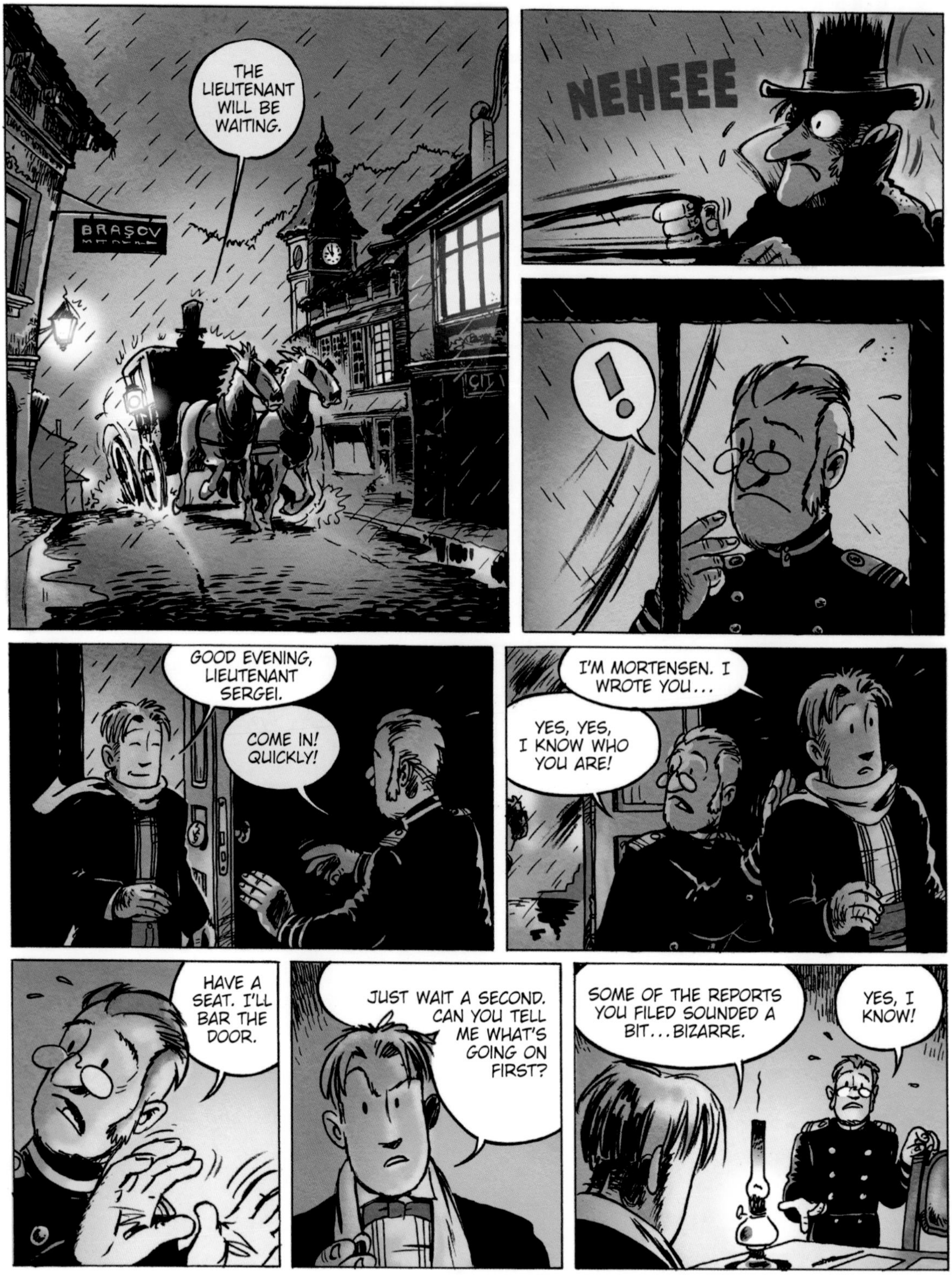
THE LIEUTENANT WILL BE WAITING.
BRAŞOV
NEHEEE
!
GOOD EVENING, LIEUTENANT SERGEI.
COME IN! QUICKLY!
I'M MORTENSEN. I WROTE YOU...
YES, YES, I KNOW WHO YOU ARE!
HAVE A SEAT. I'LL BAR THE DOOR.
JUST WAIT A SECOND. CAN YOU TELL ME WHAT'S GOING ON FIRST?
SOME OF THE REPORTS YOU FILED SOUNDED A BIT...BIZARRE.
YES, I KNOW!

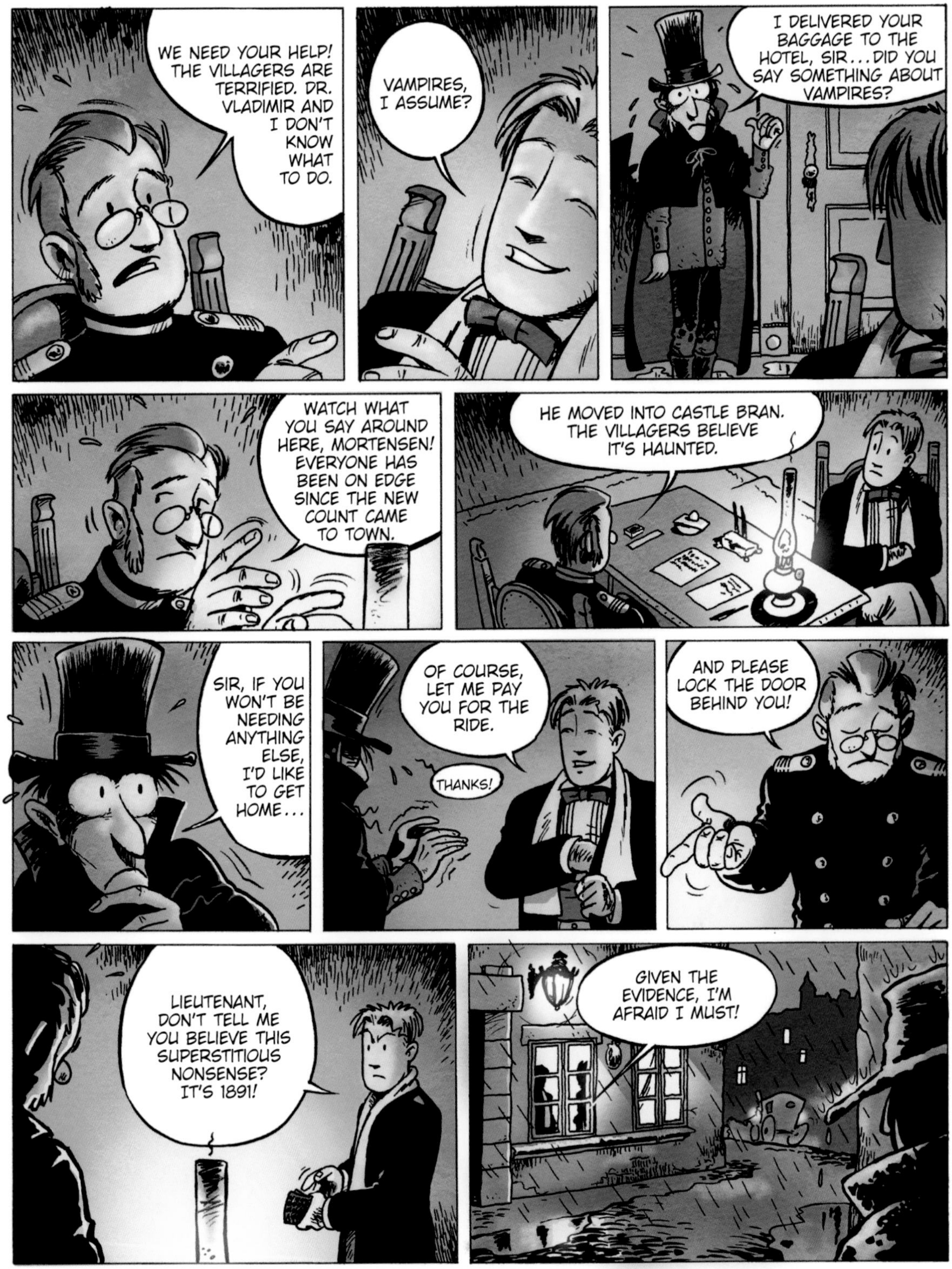
WE NEED YOUR HELP! THE VILLAGERS ARE TERRIFIED. DR. VLADIMIR AND I DON'T KNOW WHAT TO DO.
VAMPIRES, I ASSUME?
I DELIVERED YOUR BAGGAGE TO THE HOTEL, SIR...DID YOU SAY SOMETHING ABOUT VAMPIRES?
WATCH WHAT YOU SAY AROUND HERE, MORTENSEN! EVERYONE HAS BEEN ON EDGE SINCE THE NEW COUNT CAME TO TOWN.
HE MOVED INTO CASTLE BRAN. THE VILLAGERS BELIEVE IT'S HAUNTED.
SIR, IF YOU WON'T BE NEEDING ANYTHING ELSE, I'D LIKE TO GET HOME...
OF COURSE, LET ME PAY YOU FOR THE RIDE.
THANKS!
AND PLEASE LOCK THE DOOR BEHIND YOU!
LIEUTENANT, DON'T TELL ME YOU BELIEVE THIS SUPERSTITIOUS NONSENSE? IT'S 1891!
GIVEN THE EVIDENCE, I'M AFRAID I MUST!

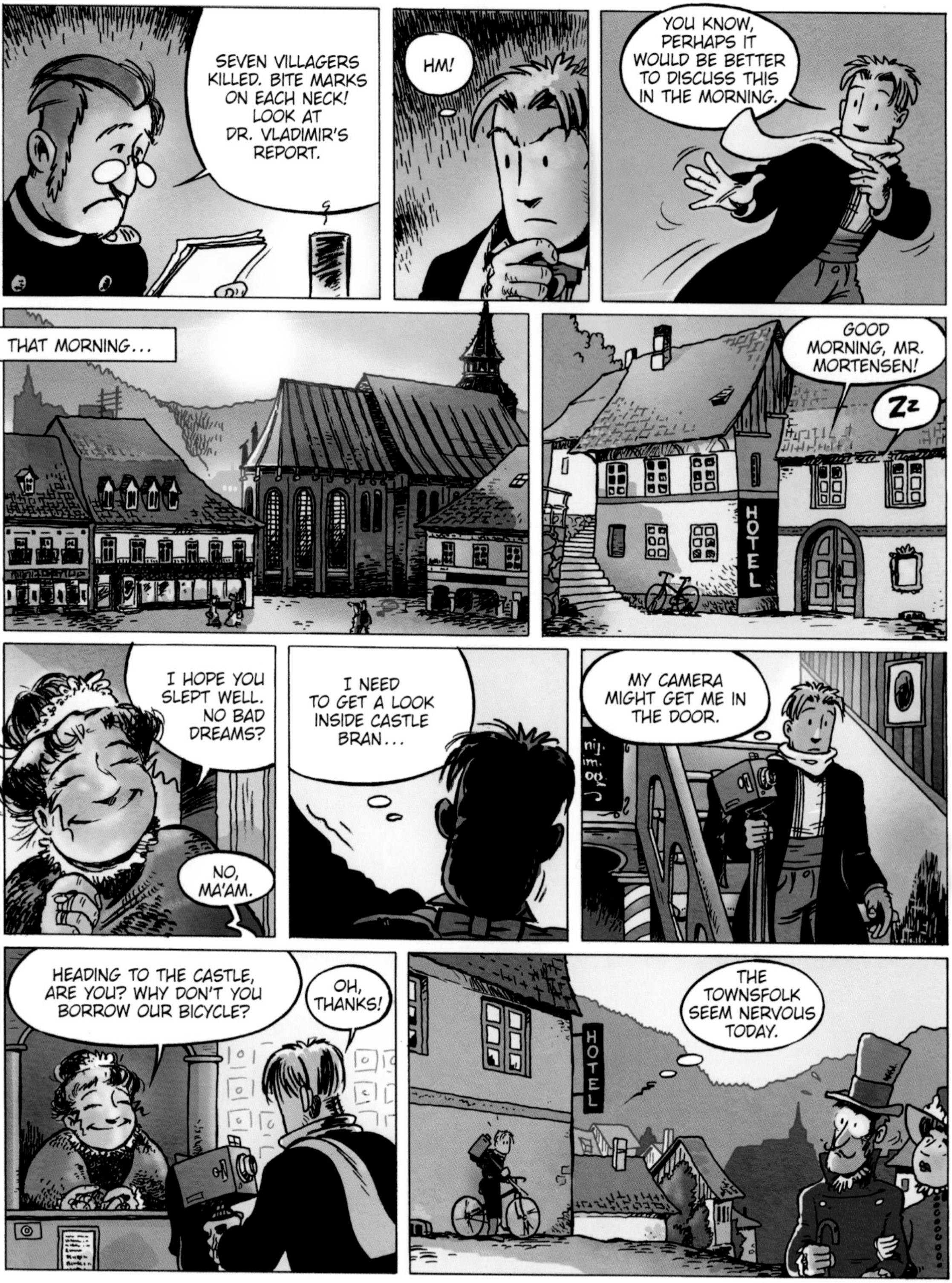
SEVEN VILLAGERS KILLED. BITE MARKS ON EACH NECK! LOOK AT DR. VLADIMIR'S REPORT.
HM!
YOU KNOW, PERHAPS IT WOULD BE BETTER TO DISCUSS THIS IN THE MORNING.
THAT MORNING...
GOOD MORNING, MR. MORTENSEN!
Zz
HOTEL
I HOPE YOU SLEPT WELL. NO BAD DREAMS?
NO, MA'AM.
I NEED TO GET A LOOK INSIDE CASTLE BRAN...
MY CAMERA MIGHT GET ME IN THE DOOR.
HEADING TO THE CASTLE, ARE YOU? WHY DON'T YOU BORROW OUR BICYCLE?
OH, THANKS!
THE TOWNSFOLK SEEM NERVOUS TODAY.
HOTEL

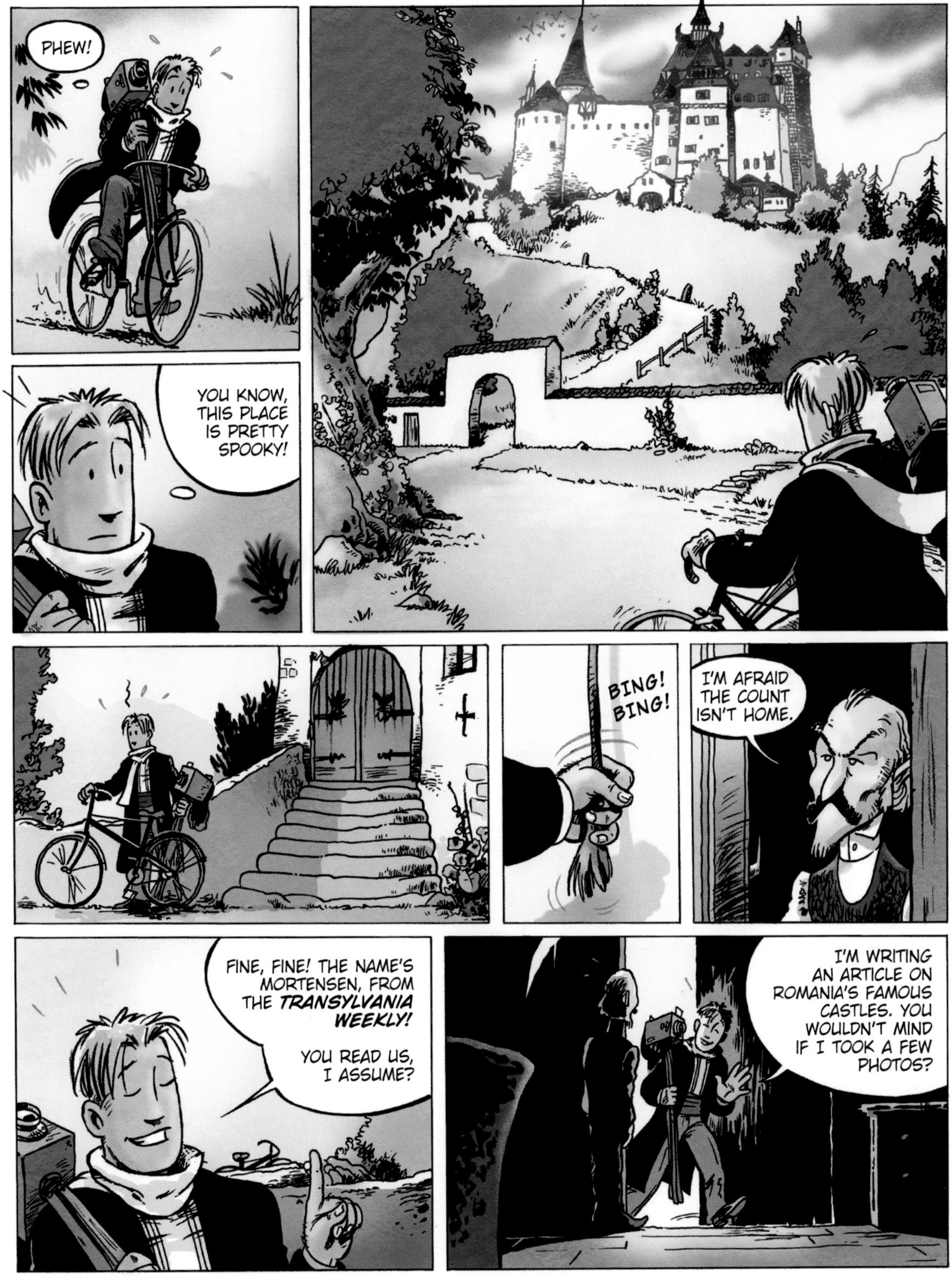
PHEW!
YOU KNOW, THIS PLACE IS PRETTY SPOOKY!
BING! BING!
I'M AFRAID THE COUNT ISN'T HOME.
FINE, FINE! THE NAME'S MORTENSEN, FROM THE TRANSYLVANIA WEEKLY!
YOU READ US, I ASSUME?
I'M WRITING AN ARTICLE ON ROMANIA'S FAMOUS CASTLES. YOU WOULDN'T MIND IF I TOOK A FEW PHOTOS?

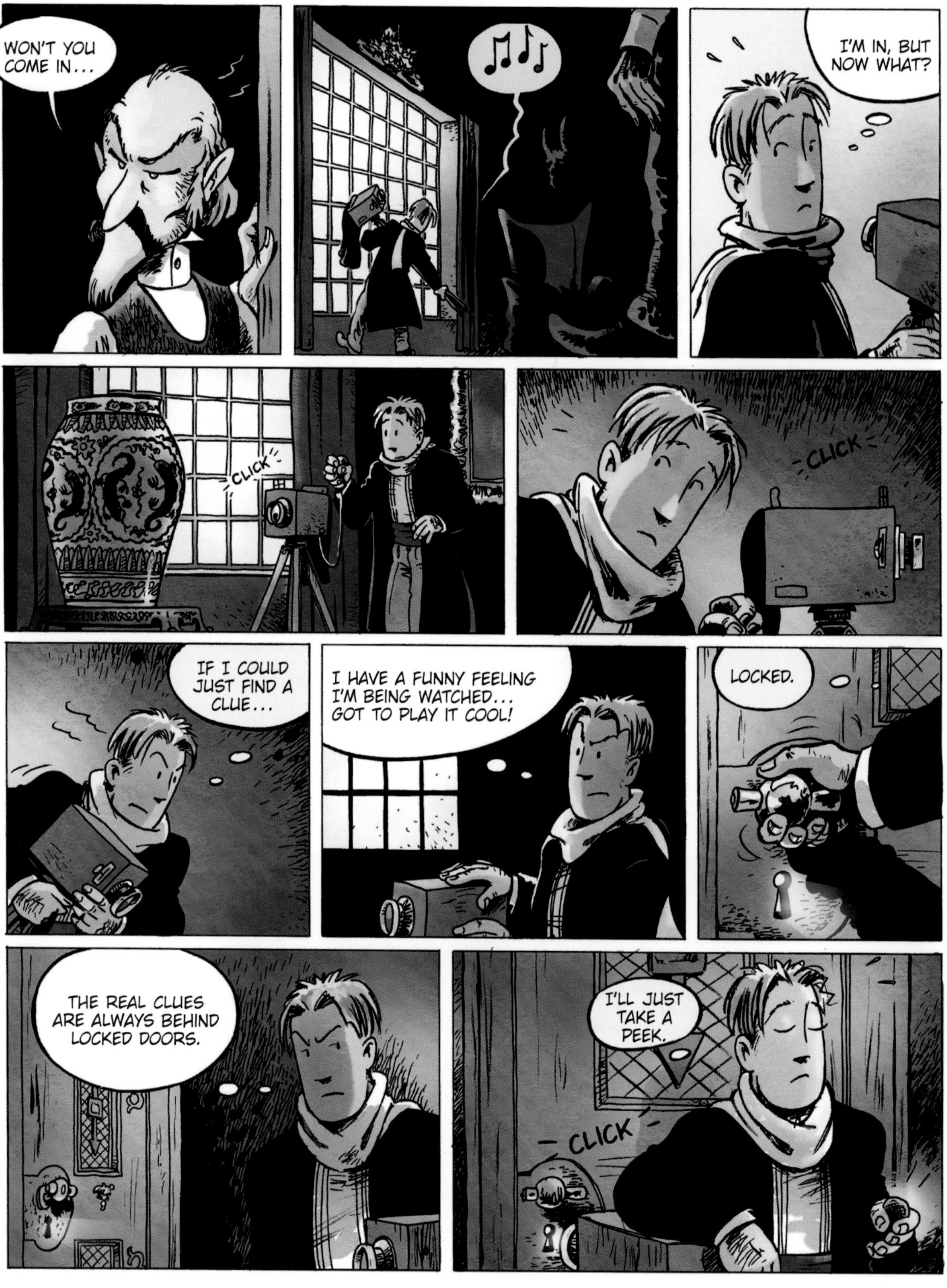
WON'T YOU COME IN...
♫♪♩
I'M IN, BUT NOW WHAT?
CLICK
CLICK
IF I COULD JUST FIND A CLUE...
I HAVE A FUNNY FEELING I'M BEING WATCHED... GOT TO PLAY IT COOL!
LOCKED.
THE REAL CLUES ARE ALWAYS BEHIND LOCKED DOORS.
I'LL JUST TAKE A PEEK.
CLICK

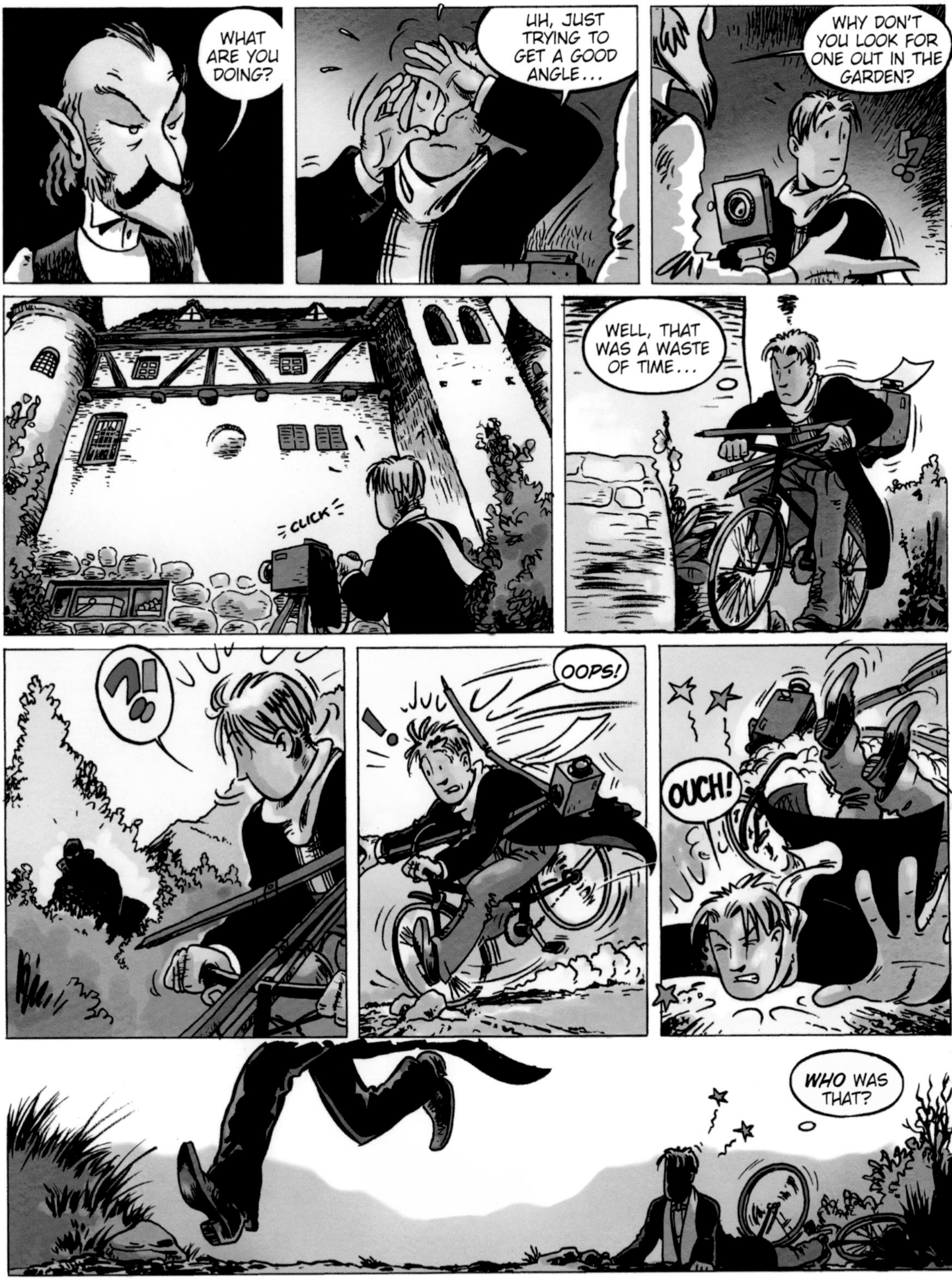
WHAT ARE YOU DOING?
UH, JUST TRYING TO GET A GOOD ANGLE...
WHY DON'T YOU LOOK FOR ONE OUT IN THE GARDEN?
CLICK
WELL, THAT WAS A WASTE OF TIME...
?!
!
OOPS!
OUCH!
WHO WAS THAT?

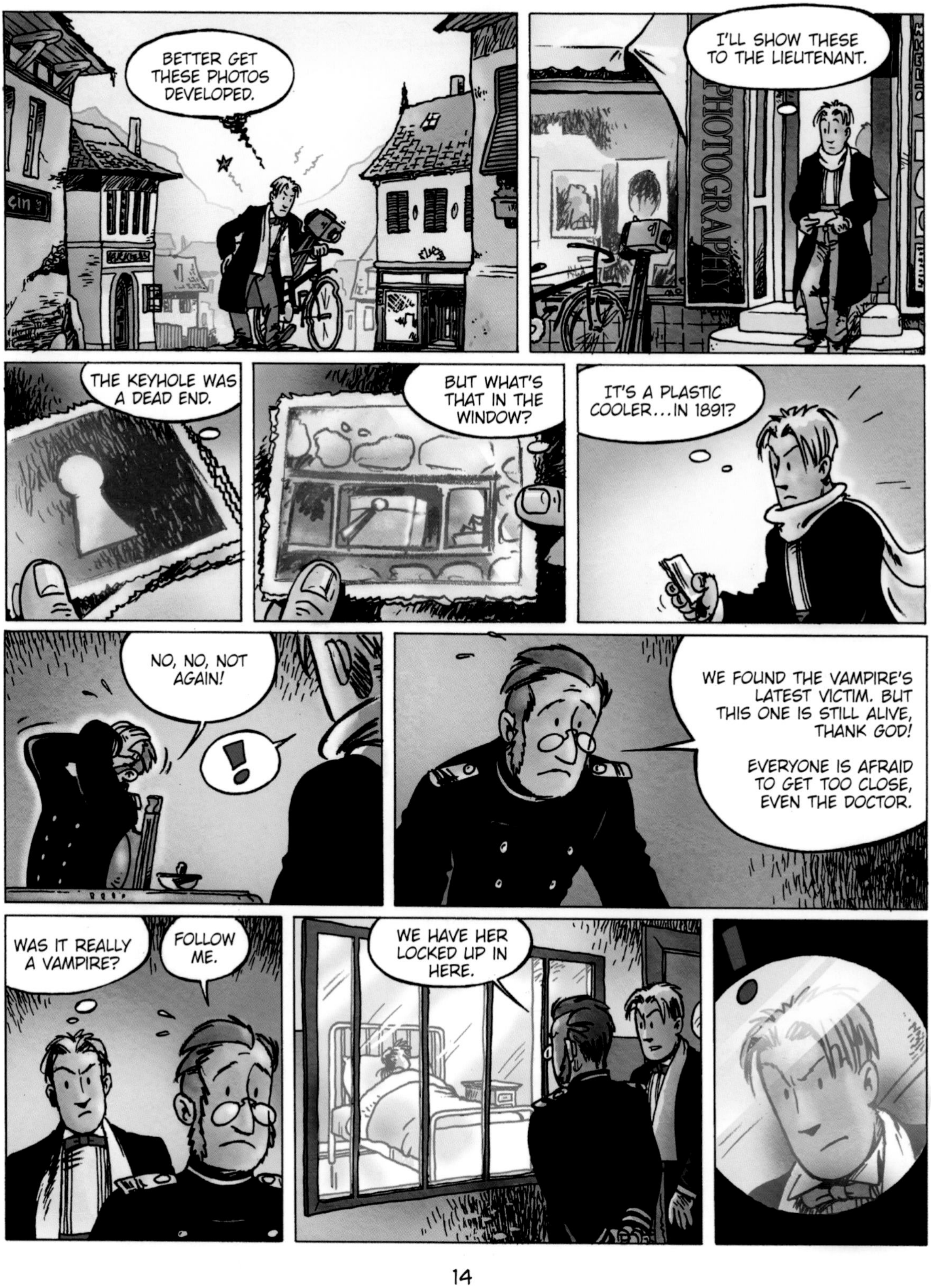
BETTER GET THESE PHOTOS DEVELOPED.
I'LL SHOW THESE TO THE LIEUTENANT.
PHOTOGRAPHY
THE KEYHOLE WAS A DEAD END.
BUT WHAT'S THAT IN THE WINDOW?
IT'S A PLASTIC COOLER...IN 1891?
NO, NO, NOT AGAIN!
!
WE FOUND THE VAMPIRE'S LATEST VICTIM. BUT THIS ONE IS STILL ALIVE, THANK GOD!
EVERYONE IS AFRAID TO GET TOO CLOSE, EVEN THE DOCTOR.
WAS IT REALLY A VAMPIRE?
FOLLOW ME.
WE HAVE HER LOCKED UP IN HERE.

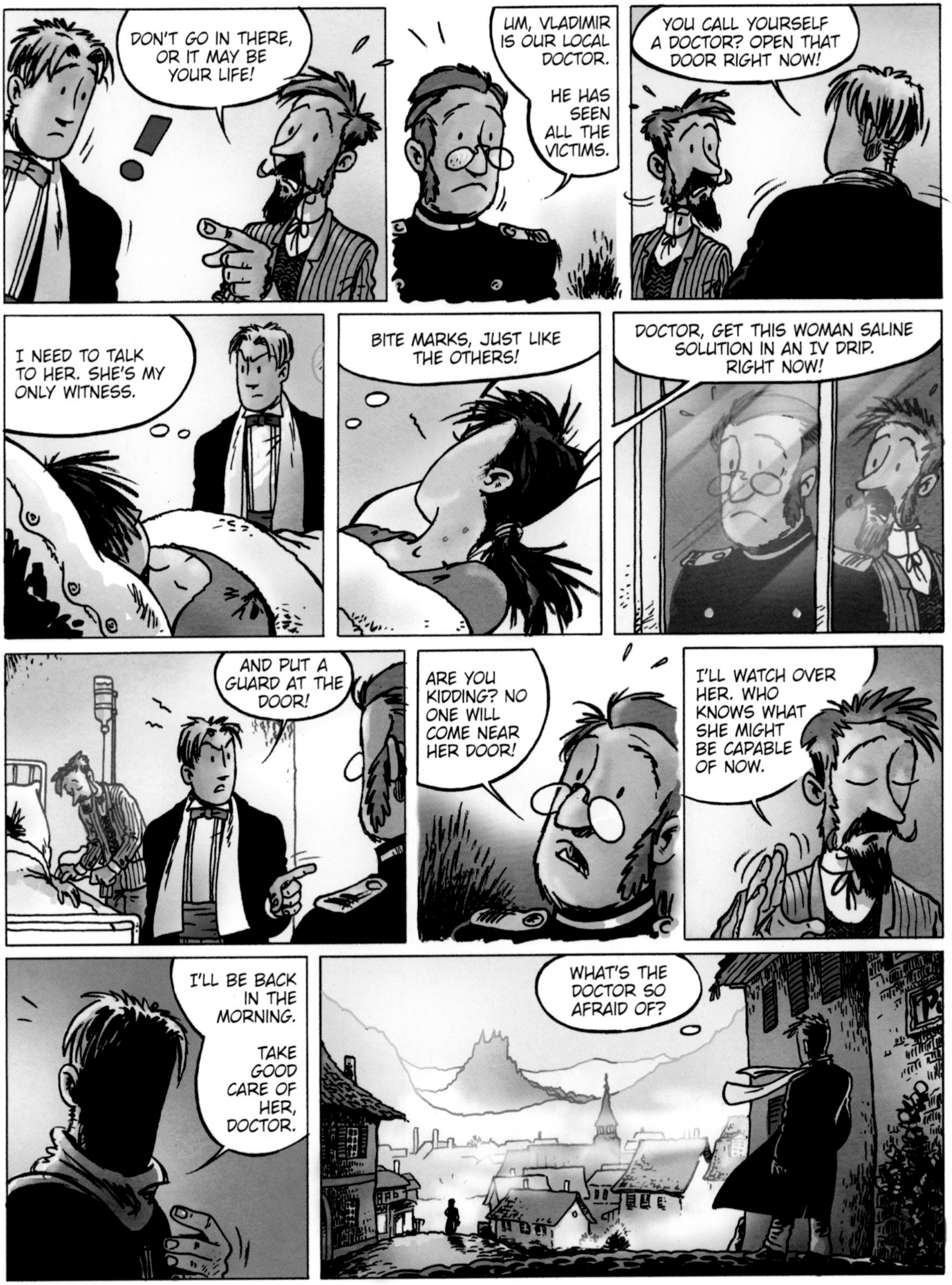
DON'T GO IN THERE, OR IT MAY BE YOUR LIFE!
UM, VLADIMIR IS OUR LOCAL DOCTOR.
HE HAS SEEN ALL THE VICTIMS.
YOU CALL YOURSELF A DOCTOR? OPEN THAT DOOR RIGHT NOW!
I NEED TO TALK TO HER. SHE'S MY ONLY WITNESS.
BITE MARKS, JUST LIKE THE OTHERS!
DOCTOR, GET THIS WOMAN SALINE SOLUTION IN AN IV DRIP. RIGHT NOW!
AND PUT A GUARD AT THE DOOR!
ARE YOU KIDDING? NO ONE WILL COME NEAR HER DOOR!
I'LL WATCH OVER HER. WHO KNOWS WHAT SHE MIGHT BE CAPABLE OF NOW.
I'LL BE BACK IN THE MORNING.
TAKE GOOD CARE OF HER, DOCTOR.
WHAT'S THE DOCTOR SO AFRAID OF?

THE NEXT MORNING...

LIEUTENANT, HOW IS SHE?

HAVE A LOOK FOR YOURSELF!

SHE DOESN'T LOOK LIKE A VAMPIRE...

MY NAME IS MORTENSEN. HOW ARE YOU FEELING TODAY?

AH, YOU'RE THE ONE WHO SAVED ME!

I'M ELENA. I'M FEELING BETTER, BUT MY SIDE STILL HURTS TERRIBLY. I GUESS THE DOCTOR STITCHED ME UP.

LOOK!

THE DOCTOR NEVER MENTIONED THIS!

WHAT HAPPENED? DO YOU REMEMBER ANYTHING?

...

I WAS TRYING TO SNEAK INTO THE CASTLE, BUT I GUESS I DIDN'T GET VERY FAR. I WAS LOOKING FOR THE COUNT, BUT I CAN'T REMEMBER WHAT HAPPENED.

HM!

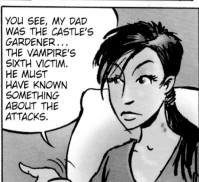
YOU SEE, MY DAD WAS THE CASTLE'S GARDENER... THE VAMPIRE'S SIXTH VICTIM. HE MUST HAVE KNOWN SOMETHING ABOUT THE ATTACKS.

I FOUND SOMETHING HIDDEN UNDER DAD'S PILLOW, AFTER HE DIED. I'M NOT SURE WHAT IT IS OR HOW HE GOT IT.

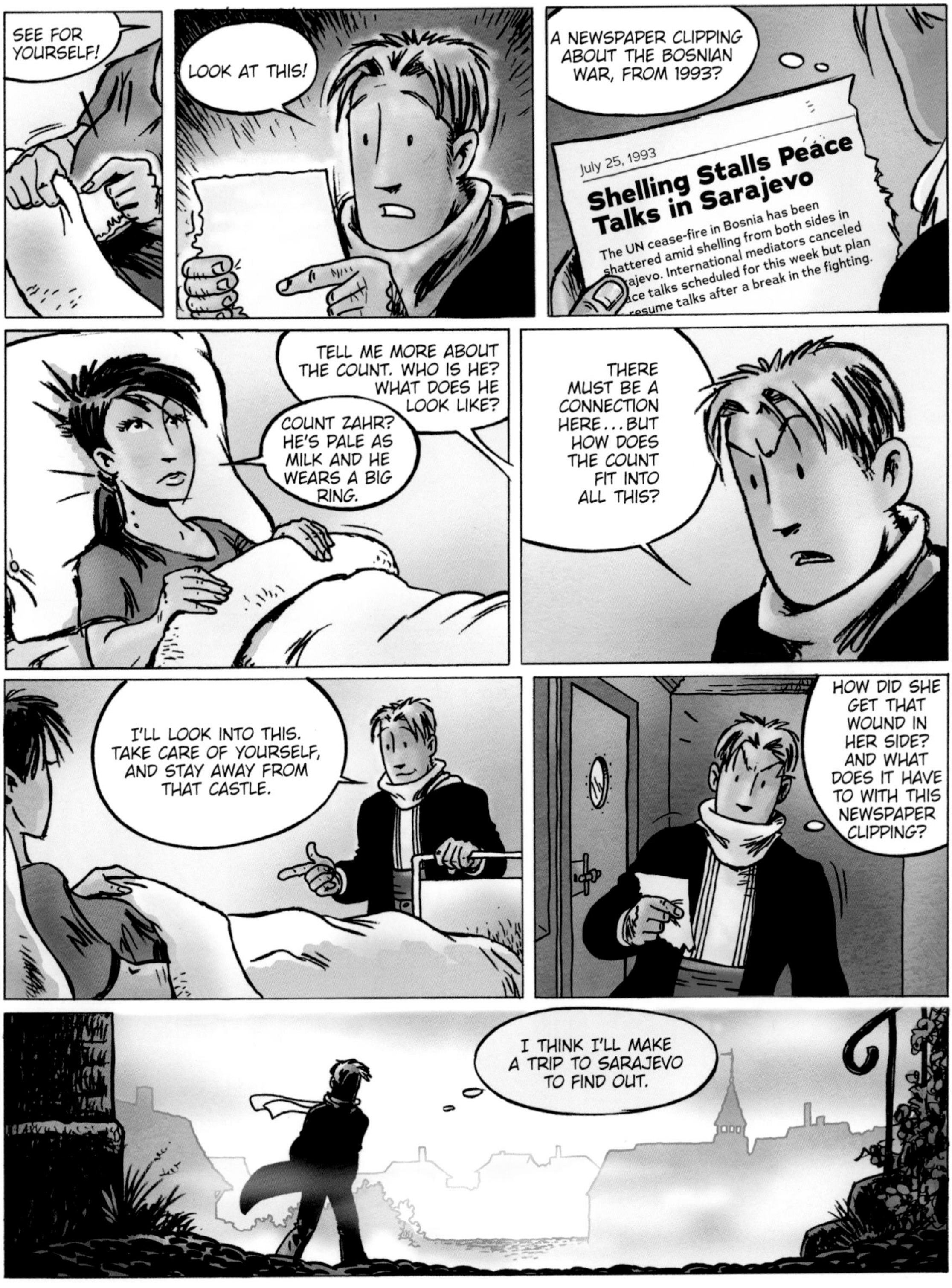
SEE FOR YOURSELF!
LOOK AT THIS!
A NEWSPAPER CLIPPING ABOUT THE BOSNIAN WAR, FROM 1993?
July 25, 1993
Shelling Stalls Peace Talks in Sarajevo
The UN cease-fire in Bosnia has been shattered amid shelling from both sides in
International mediators canceled
talks scheduled for this week but plan
resume talks after a break in the fighting.
TELL ME MORE ABOUT THE COUNT. WHO IS HE? WHAT DOES HE LOOK LIKE?
COUNT ZAHR? HE'S PALE AS MILK AND HE WEARS A BIG RING.
THERE MUST BE A CONNECTION HERE... BUT HOW DOES THE COUNT FIT INTO ALL THIS?
I'LL LOOK INTO THIS. TAKE CARE OF YOURSELF, AND STAY AWAY FROM THAT CASTLE.
HOW DID SHE GET THAT WOUND IN HER SIDE? AND WHAT DOES IT HAVE TO WITH THIS NEWSPAPER CLIPPING?
I THINK I'LL MAKE A TRIP TO SARAJEVO TO FIND OUT.

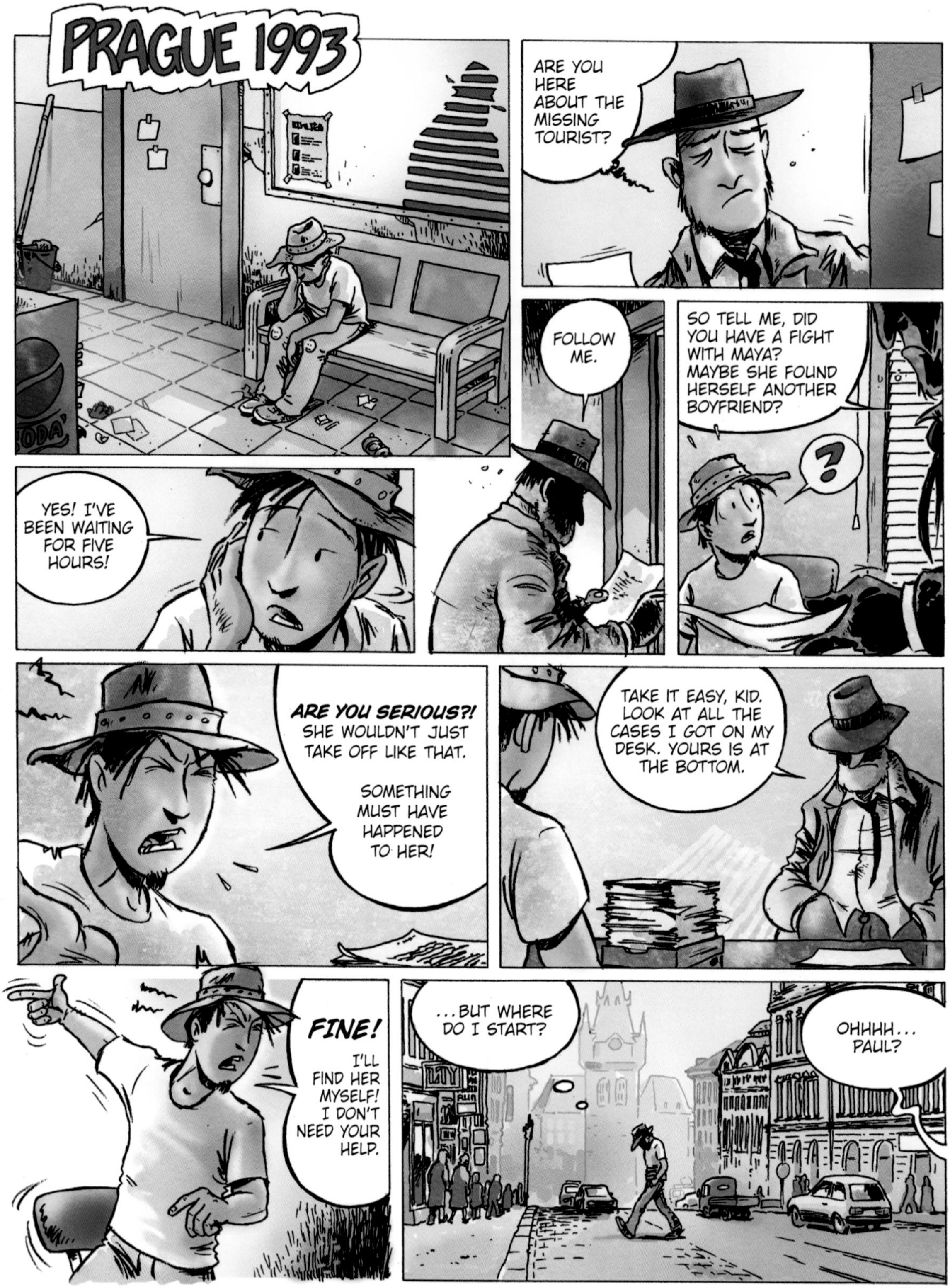
PRAGUE 1993
ARE YOU HERE ABOUT THE MISSING TOURIST?
YES! I'VE BEEN WAITING FOR FIVE HOURS!
FOLLOW ME.
SO TELL ME, DID YOU HAVE A FIGHT WITH MAYA? MAYBE SHE FOUND HERSELF ANOTHER BOYFRIEND?
?
ARE YOU SERIOUS?! SHE WOULDN'T JUST TAKE OFF LIKE THAT.
SOMETHING MUST HAVE HAPPENED TO HER!
TAKE IT EASY, KID. LOOK AT ALL THE CASES I GOT ON MY DESK. YOURS IS AT THE BOTTOM.
FINE!
I'LL FIND HER MYSELF! I DON'T NEED YOUR HELP.
...BUT WHERE DO I START?
OHHHH... PAUL?

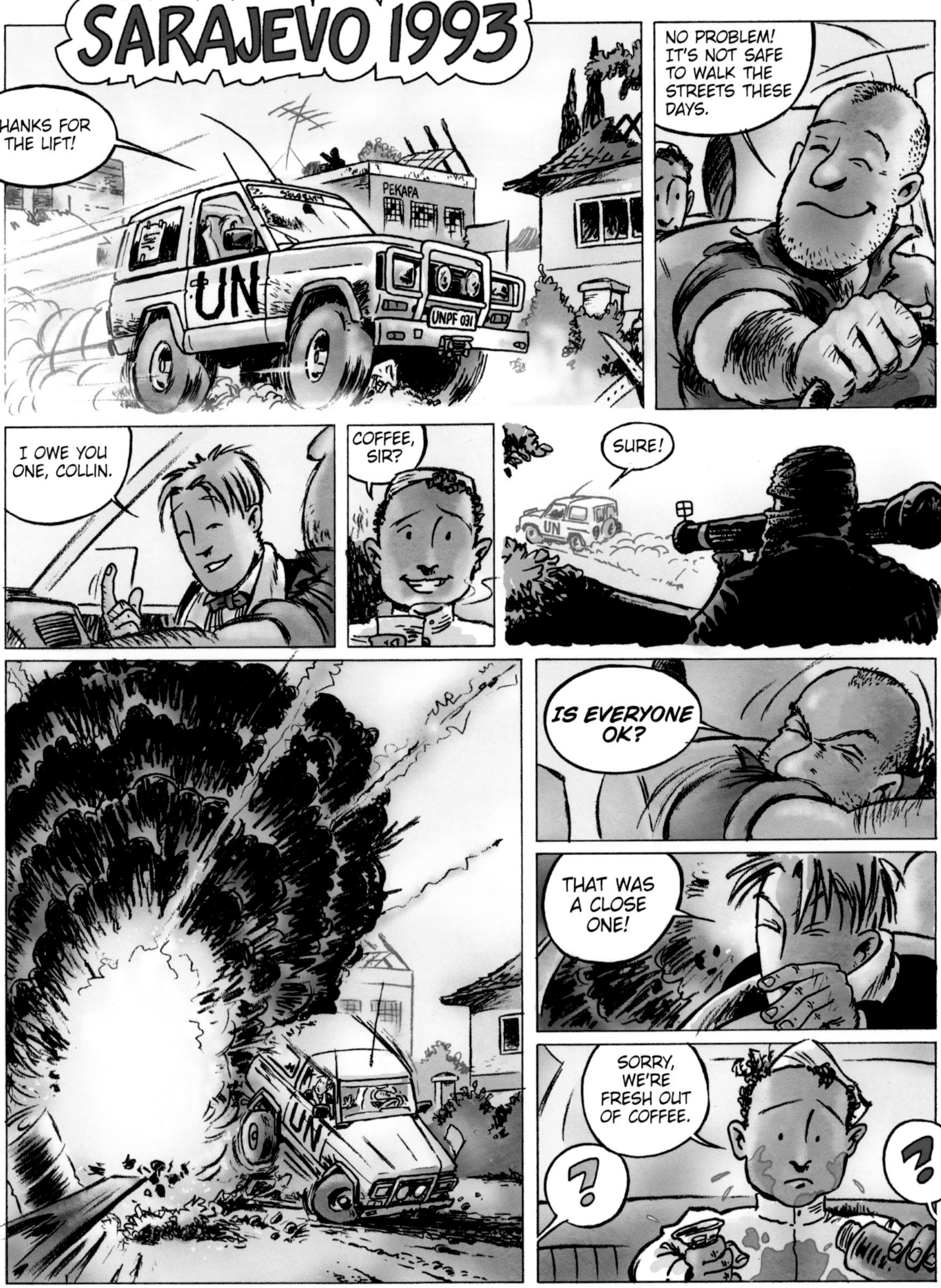
SARAJEVO 1993
THANKS FOR THE LIFT!
PEKAPA
UN
UNPF 031
NO PROBLEM! IT'S NOT SAFE TO WALK THE STREETS THESE DAYS.
I OWE YOU ONE, COLLIN.
COFFEE, SIR?
SURE!
UN
UN
IS EVERYONE OK?
THAT WAS A CLOSE ONE!
SORRY, WE'RE FRESH OUT OF COFFEE.
?
?

THE IMPORTANT THING IS WE'RE SAFE. TENSIONS ARE HIGH. THE PEACE NEGOTIATIONS ARE NOT GOING SMOOTHLY.

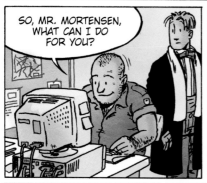

SO, MR. MORTENSEN, WHAT CAN I DO FOR YOU?

CAN YOU POINT ME TO THE PEACE TALKS?

THE PEACE TALKS? ARE YOU ONE OF THE... MEDIATORS?

WELL, NO. BUT I'D LIKE TO OBSERVE.

OK, GOOD! I'M DOING SECURITY AT THE MEETING. I'LL GET YOU IN.

...FAX THIS REPORT TO HEADQUARTERS, SAJI!

THESE "PEACE NEGOTIATIONS" ARE JUST AN EXCUSE FOR CORRUPT OFFICIALS TO DO BUSINESS WITH EACH OTHER.

WHAT? BUT IF...

SIR? THE FAX ISN'T WORKING.

SAJI, THAT'S THE PAPER SHREDDER!

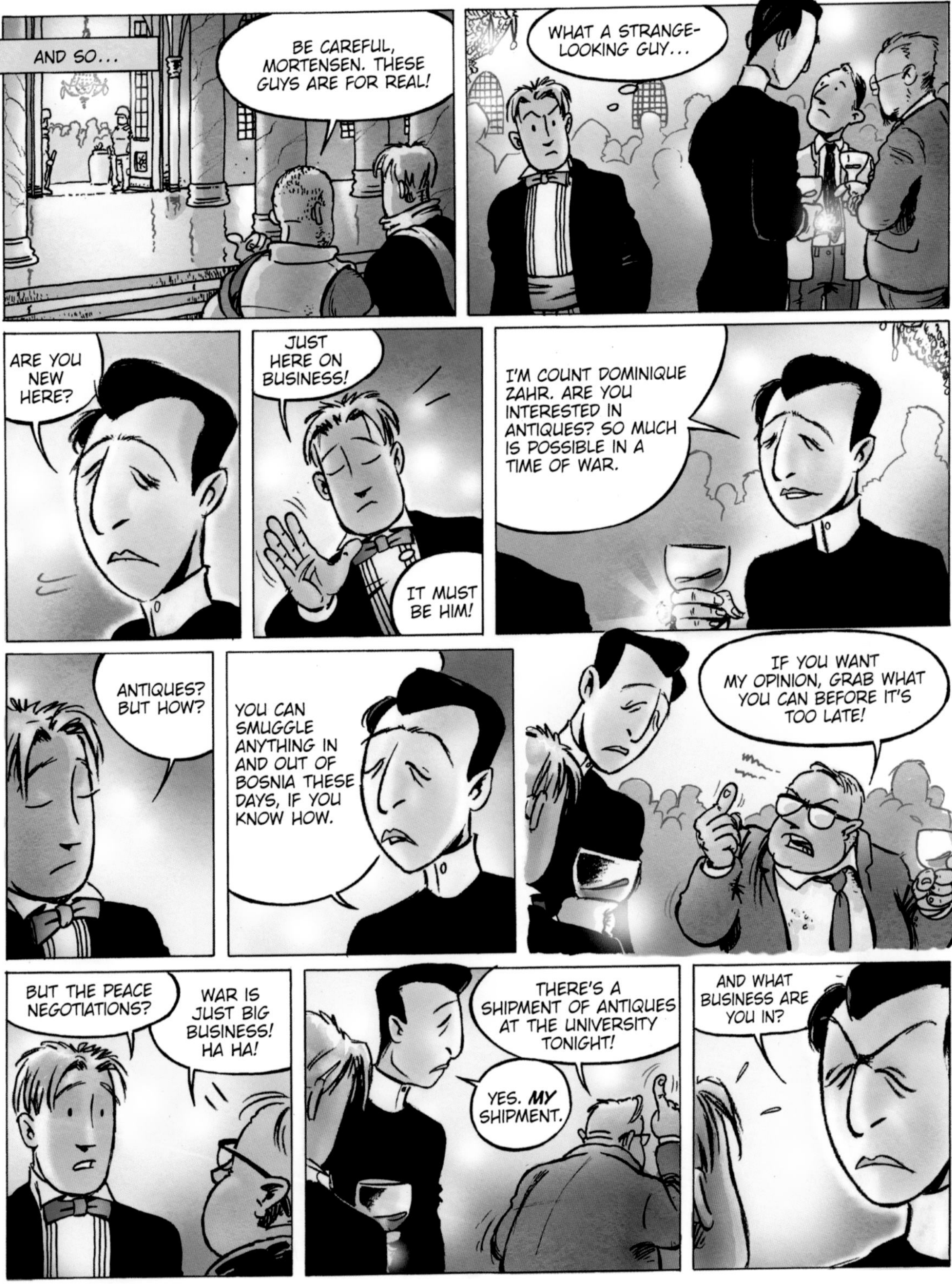
AND SO...
BE CAREFUL, MORTENSEN. THESE GUYS ARE FOR REAL!
WHAT A STRANGE-LOOKING GUY...
ARE YOU NEW HERE?
JUST HERE ON BUSINESS!
IT MUST BE HIM!
I'M COUNT DOMINIQUE ZAHR. ARE YOU INTERESTED IN ANTIQUES? SO MUCH IS POSSIBLE IN A TIME OF WAR.
ANTIQUES? BUT HOW?
YOU CAN SMUGGLE ANYTHING IN AND OUT OF BOSNIA THESE DAYS, IF YOU KNOW HOW.
IF YOU WANT MY OPINION, GRAB WHAT YOU CAN BEFORE IT'S TOO LATE!
BUT THE PEACE NEGOTIATIONS?
WAR IS JUST BIG BUSINESS! HA HA!
THERE'S A SHIPMENT OF ANTIQUES AT THE UNIVERSITY TONIGHT!
YES. ***MY*** SHIPMENT.
AND WHAT BUSINESS ARE YOU IN?

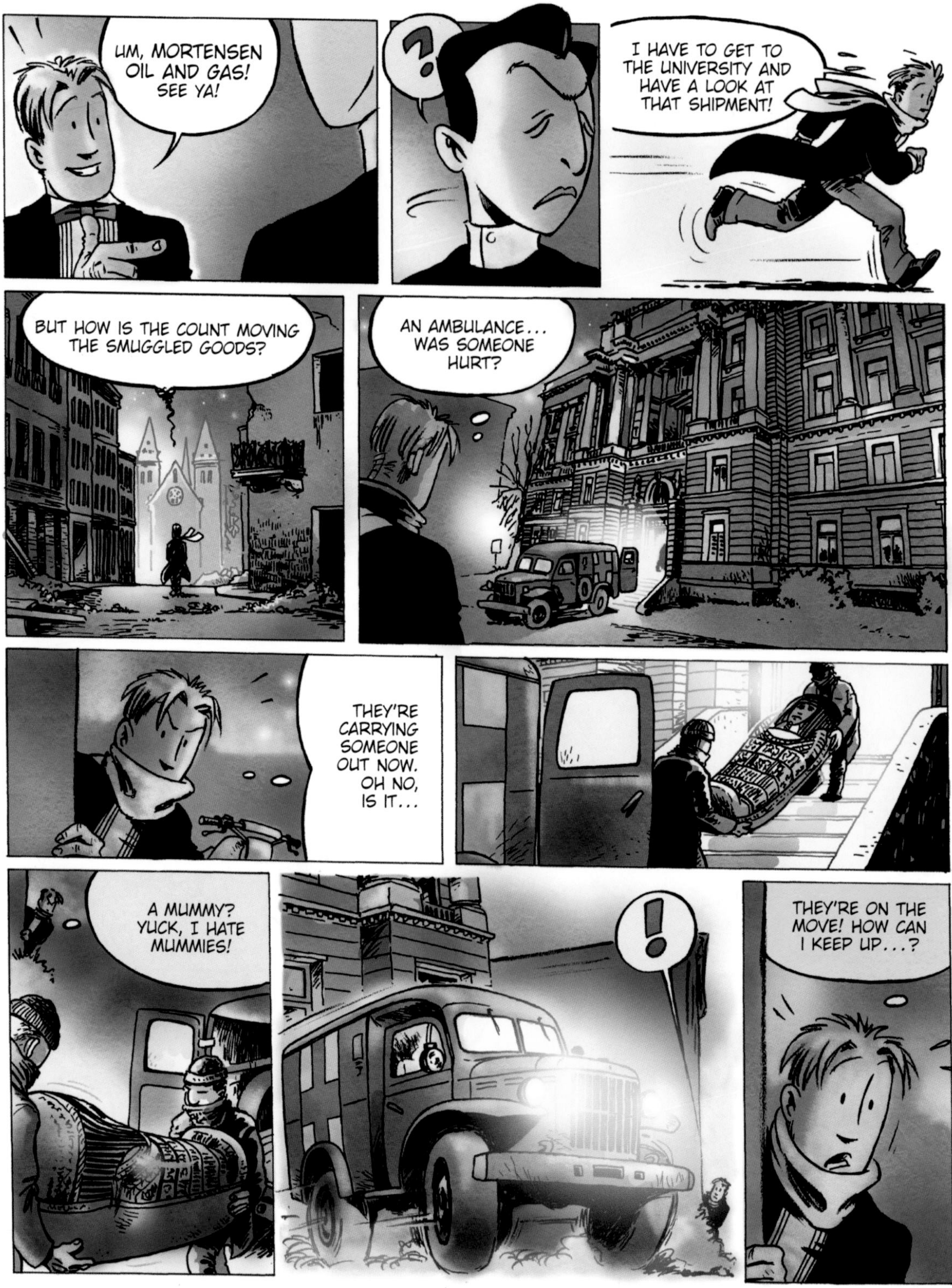
UM, MORTENSEN OIL AND GAS! SEE YA!
?
I HAVE TO GET TO THE UNIVERSITY AND HAVE A LOOK AT THAT SHIPMENT!
BUT HOW IS THE COUNT MOVING THE SMUGGLED GOODS?
AN AMBULANCE... WAS SOMEONE HURT?
THEY'RE CARRYING SOMEONE OUT NOW. OH NO, IS IT...
A MUMMY? YUCK, I HATE MUMMIES!
!
THEY'RE ON THE MOVE! HOW CAN I KEEP UP...?

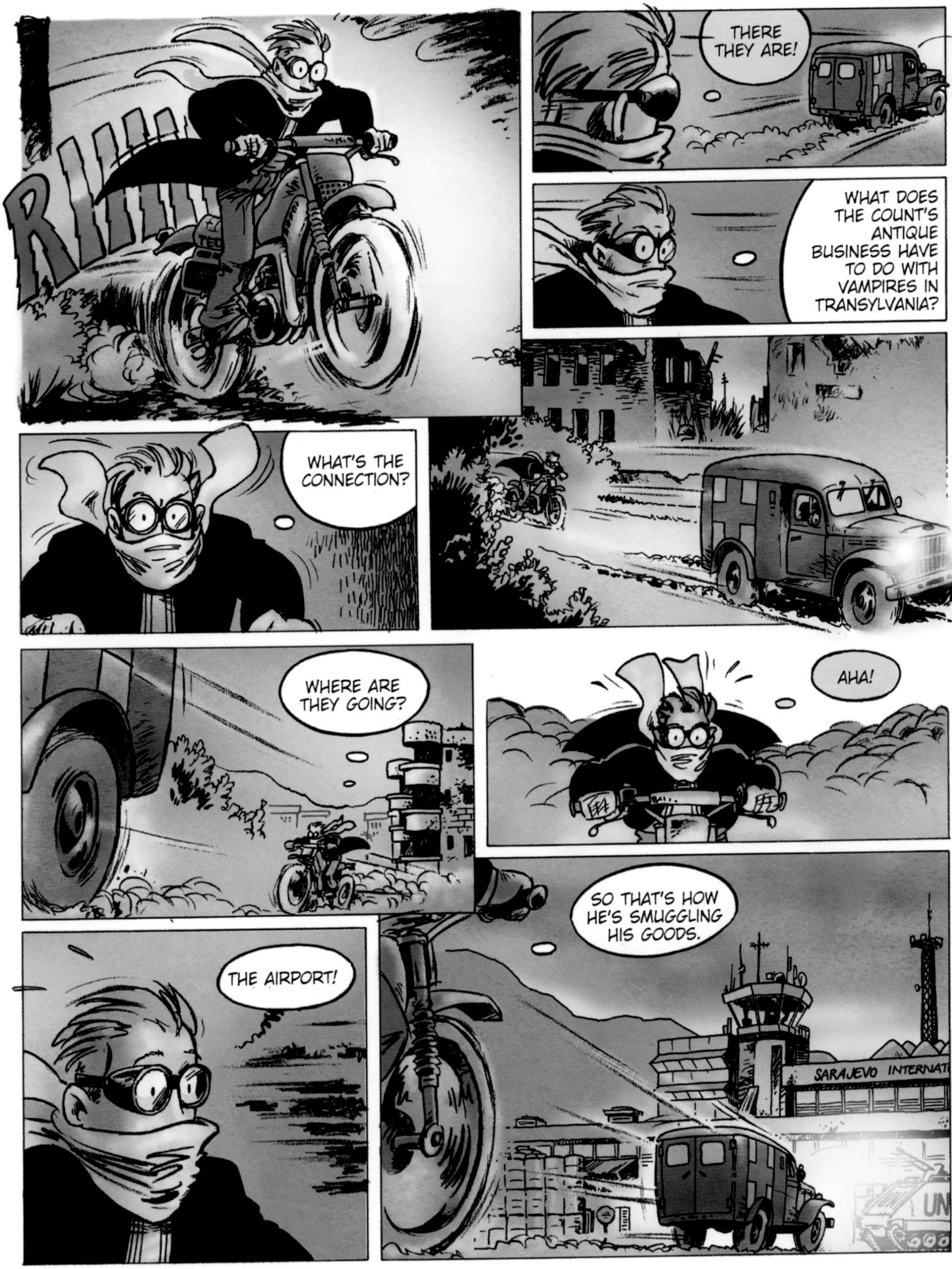
RHHH
THERE THEY ARE!
WHAT DOES THE COUNT'S ANTIQUE BUSINESS HAVE TO DO WITH VAMPIRES IN TRANSYLVANIA?
WHAT'S THE CONNECTION?
WHERE ARE THEY GOING?
AHA!
THE AIRPORT!
SO THAT'S HOW HE'S SMUGGLING HIS GOODS.
SARAJEVO INTERNAT
UN

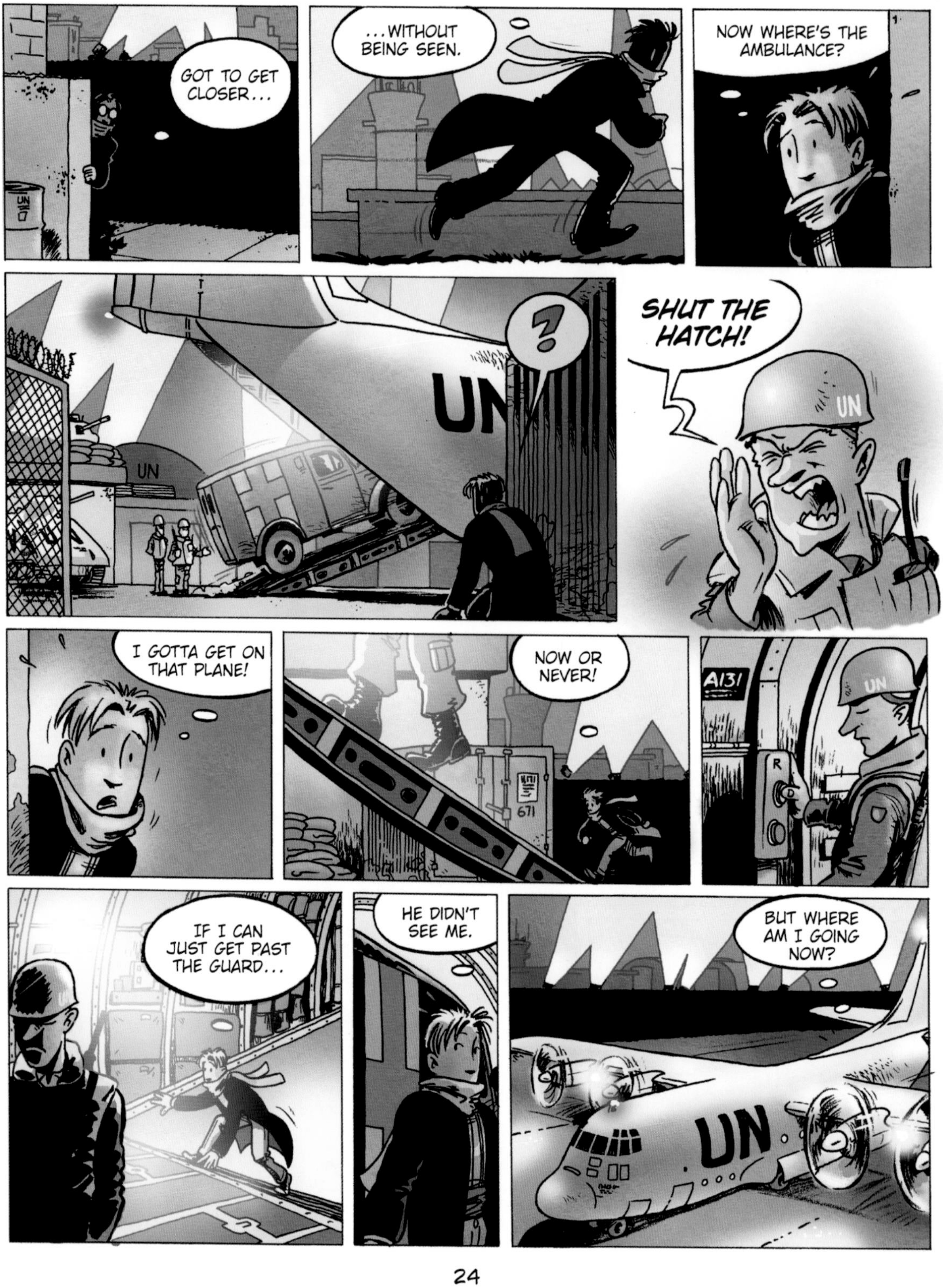
GOT TO GET CLOSER...
...WITHOUT BEING SEEN.
NOW WHERE'S THE AMBULANCE?
UN
UN
?
SHUT THE HATCH!
UN
I GOTTA GET ON THAT PLANE!
NOW OR NEVER!
671
A131
UN
IF I CAN JUST GET PAST THE GUARD...
HE DIDN'T SEE ME.
BUT WHERE AM I GOING NOW?
UN

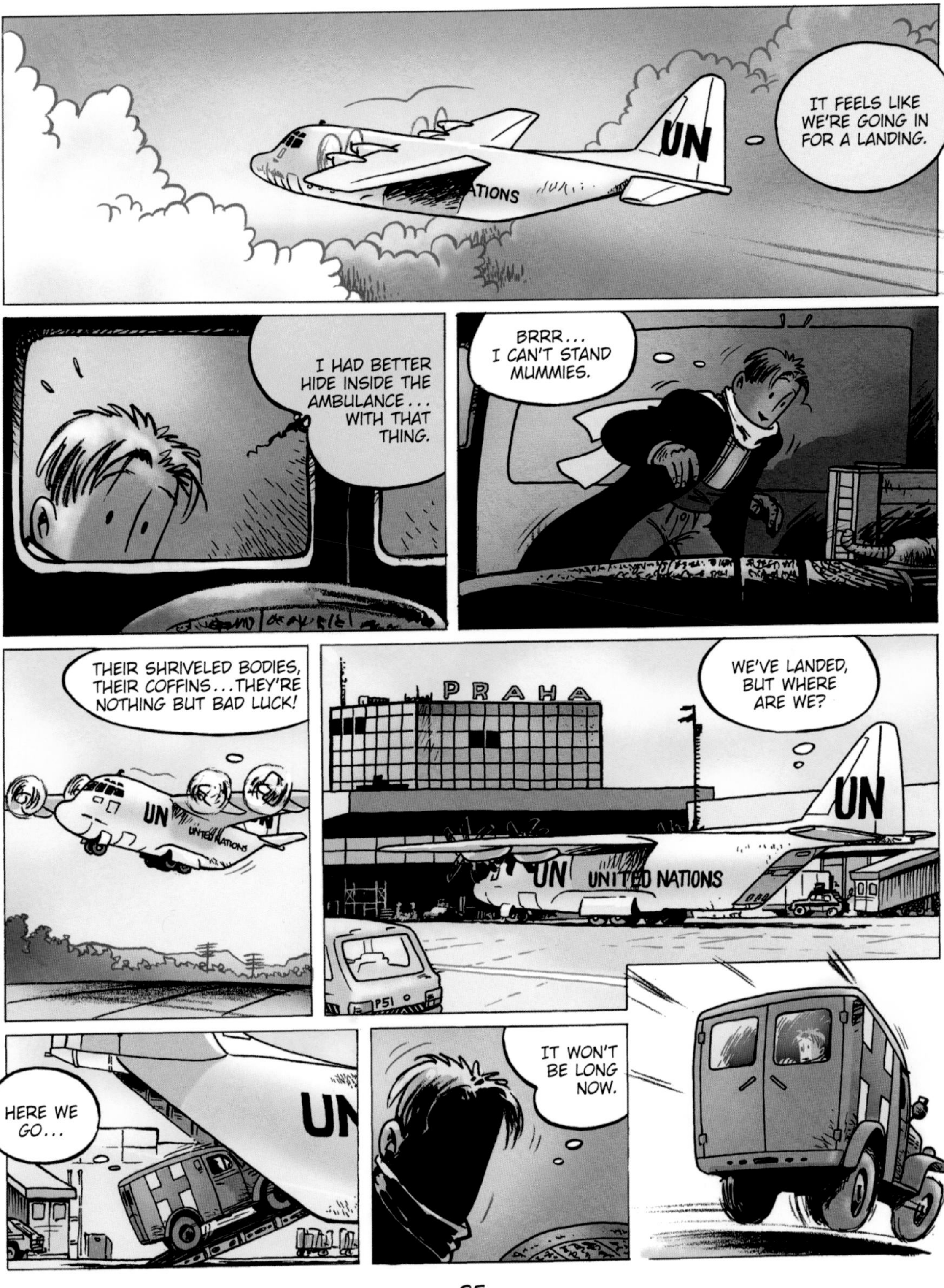
UN
...ATIONS
IT FEELS LIKE WE'RE GOING IN FOR A LANDING.
I HAD BETTER HIDE INSIDE THE AMBULANCE... WITH THAT THING.
BRRR... I CAN'T STAND MUMMIES.
THEIR SHRIVELED BODIES, THEIR COFFINS...THEY'RE NOTHING BUT BAD LUCK!
UN
PRAHA
WE'VE LANDED, BUT WHERE ARE WE?
UN
UN UNITED NATIONS
P51
HERE WE GO...
UN
IT WON'T BE LONG NOW.

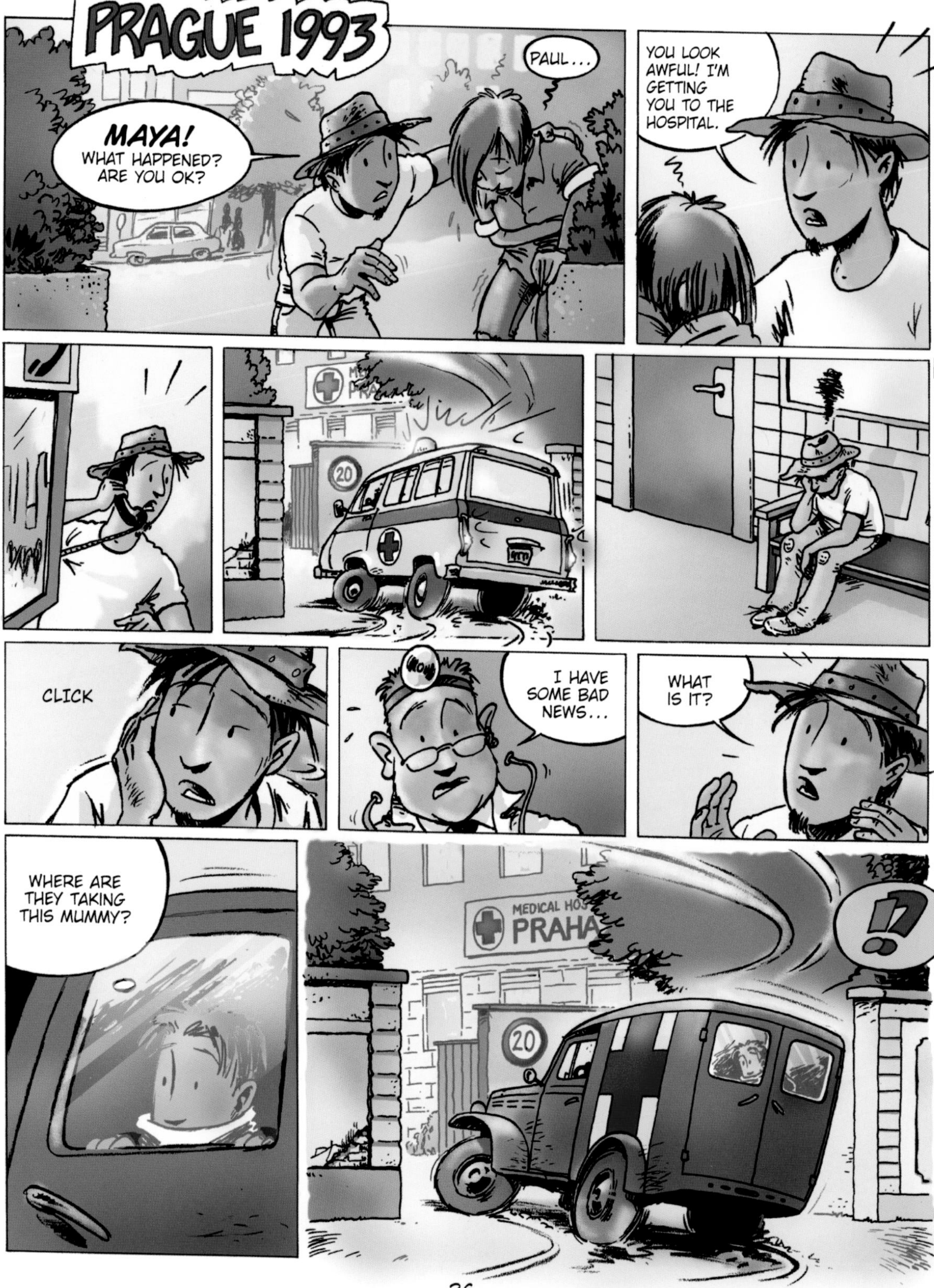
PRAGUE 1993
MAYA! WHAT HAPPENED? ARE YOU OK?
PAUL...
YOU LOOK AWFUL! I'M GETTING YOU TO THE HOSPITAL.
MEDICAL HOS
PRAHA
20
CLICK
I HAVE SOME BAD NEWS...
WHAT IS IT?
WHERE ARE THEY TAKING THIS MUMMY?

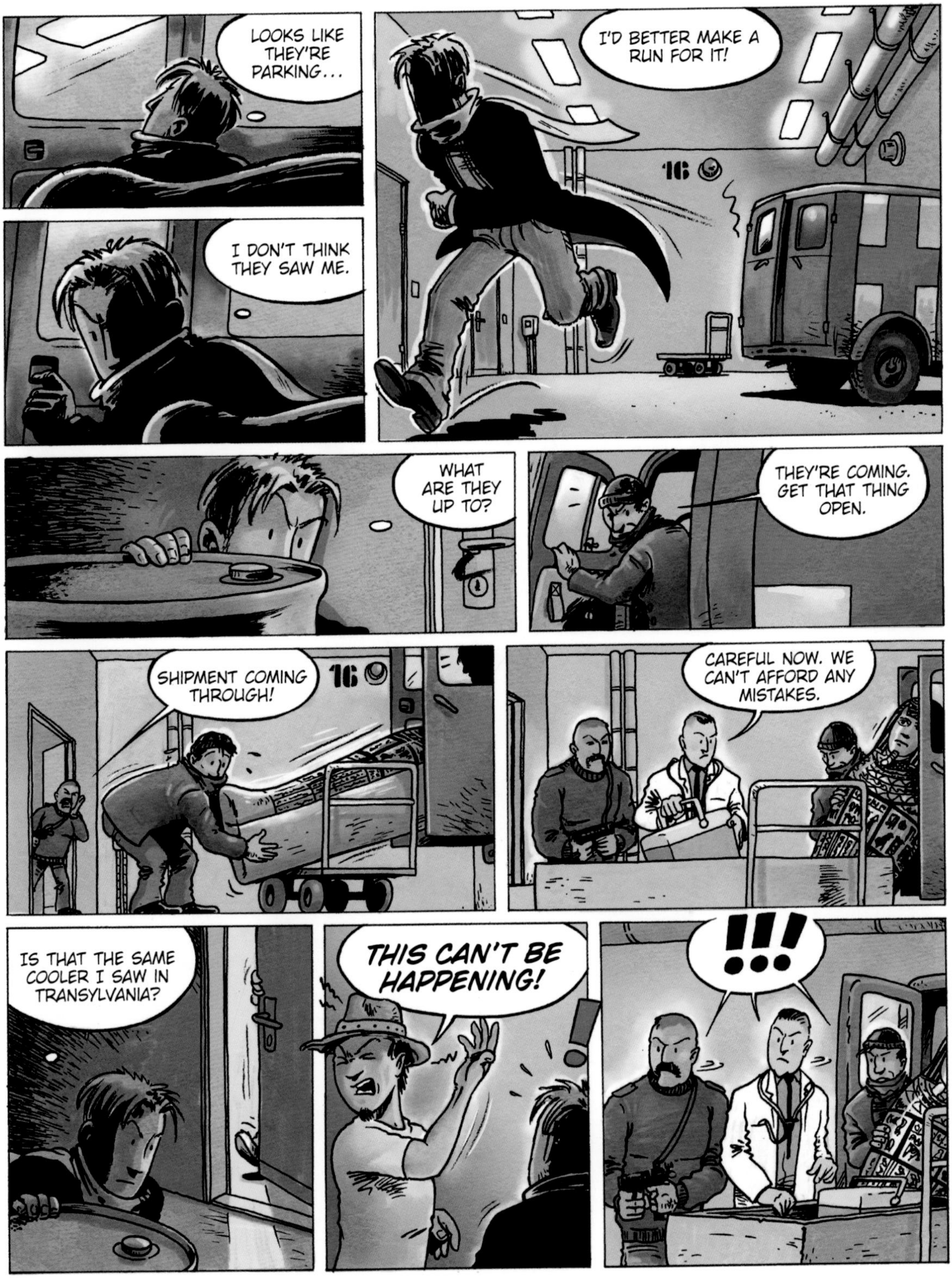
LOOKS LIKE THEY'RE PARKING...
I'D BETTER MAKE A RUN FOR IT!
16
I DON'T THINK THEY SAW ME.
WHAT ARE THEY UP TO?
THEY'RE COMING. GET THAT THING OPEN.
SHIPMENT COMING THROUGH!
16
CAREFUL NOW. WE CAN'T AFFORD ANY MISTAKES.
IS THAT THE SAME COOLER I SAW IN TRANSYLVANIA?
THIS CAN'T BE HAPPENING!
!
!!!

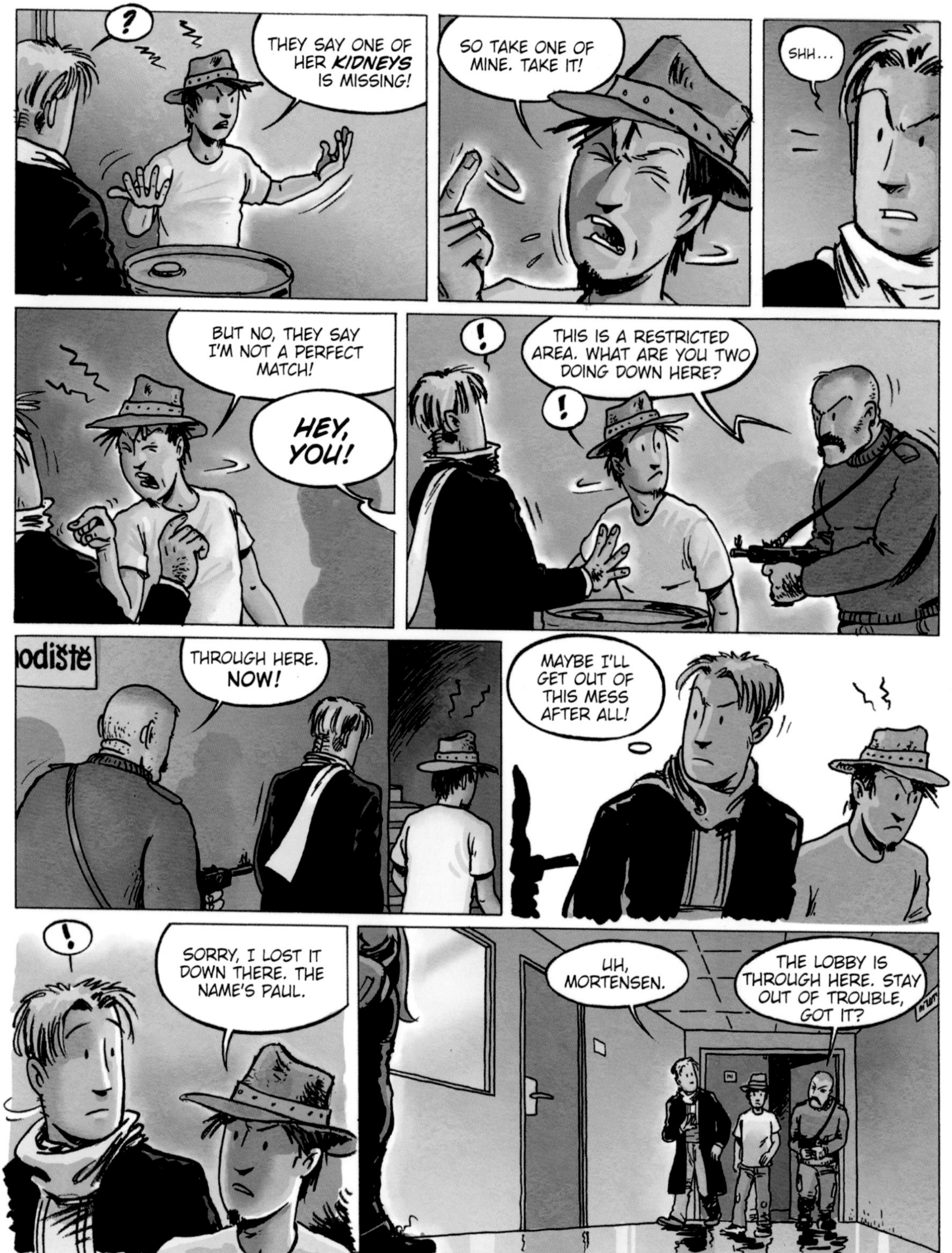
?
THEY SAY ONE OF HER KIDNEYS IS MISSING!
SO TAKE ONE OF MINE. TAKE IT!
SHH...
BUT NO, THEY SAY I'M NOT A PERFECT MATCH!
HEY, YOU!
!
THIS IS A RESTRICTED AREA. WHAT ARE YOU TWO DOING DOWN HERE?
!
odiště
THROUGH HERE. NOW!
MAYBE I'LL GET OUT OF THIS MESS AFTER ALL!
!
SORRY, I LOST IT DOWN THERE. THE NAME'S PAUL.
UH, MORTENSEN.
THE LOBBY IS THROUGH HERE. STAY OUT OF TROUBLE, GOT IT?

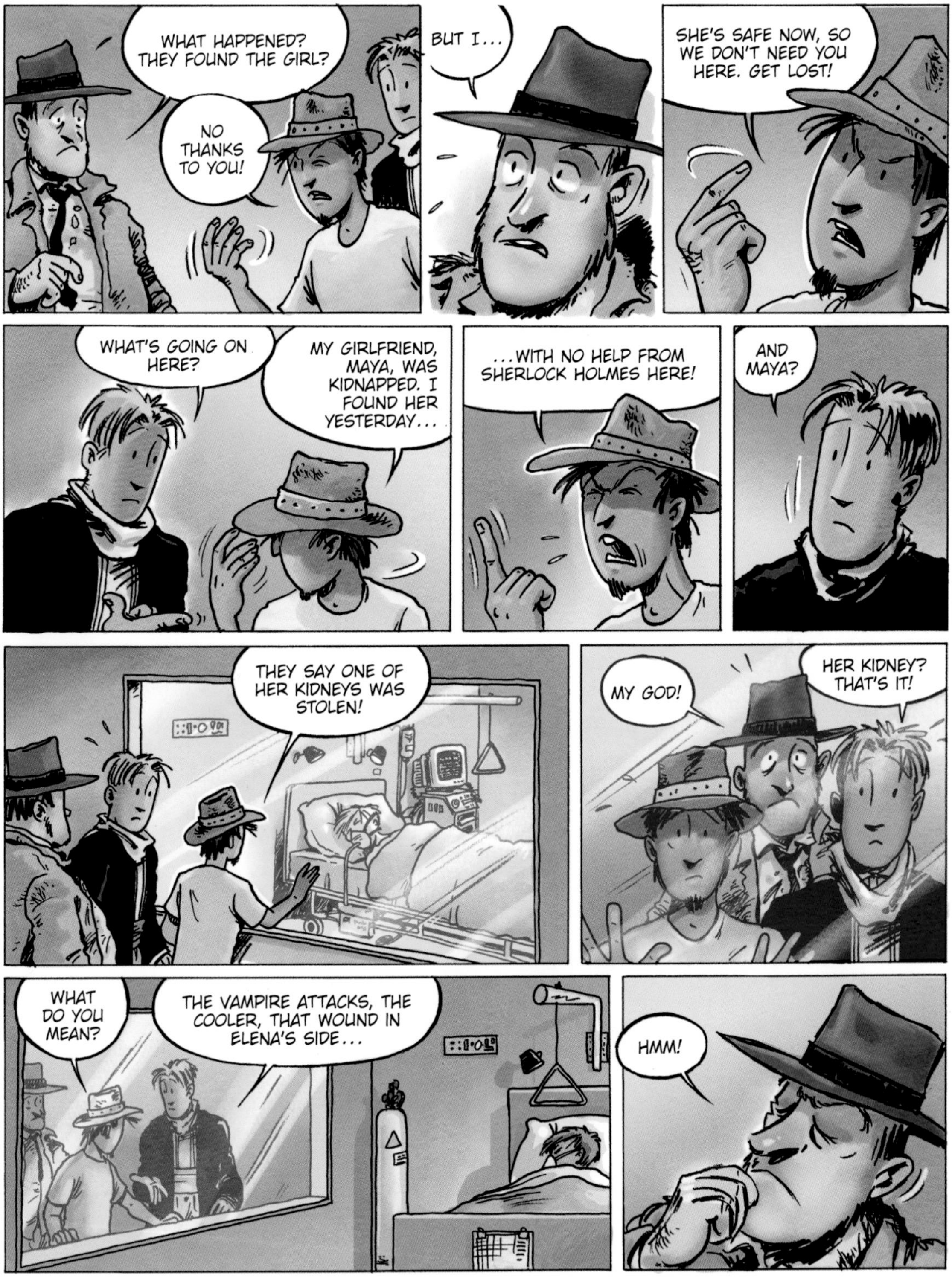
WHAT HAPPENED? THEY FOUND THE GIRL?
NO THANKS TO YOU!
BUT I...
SHE'S SAFE NOW, SO WE DON'T NEED YOU HERE. GET LOST!
WHAT'S GOING ON HERE?
MY GIRLFRIEND, MAYA, WAS KIDNAPPED. I FOUND HER YESTERDAY...
...WITH NO HELP FROM SHERLOCK HOLMES HERE!
AND MAYA?
THEY SAY ONE OF HER KIDNEYS WAS STOLEN!
MY GOD!
HER KIDNEY? THAT'S IT!
WHAT DO YOU MEAN?
THE VAMPIRE ATTACKS, THE COOLER, THAT WOUND IN ELENA'S SIDE...
HMM!

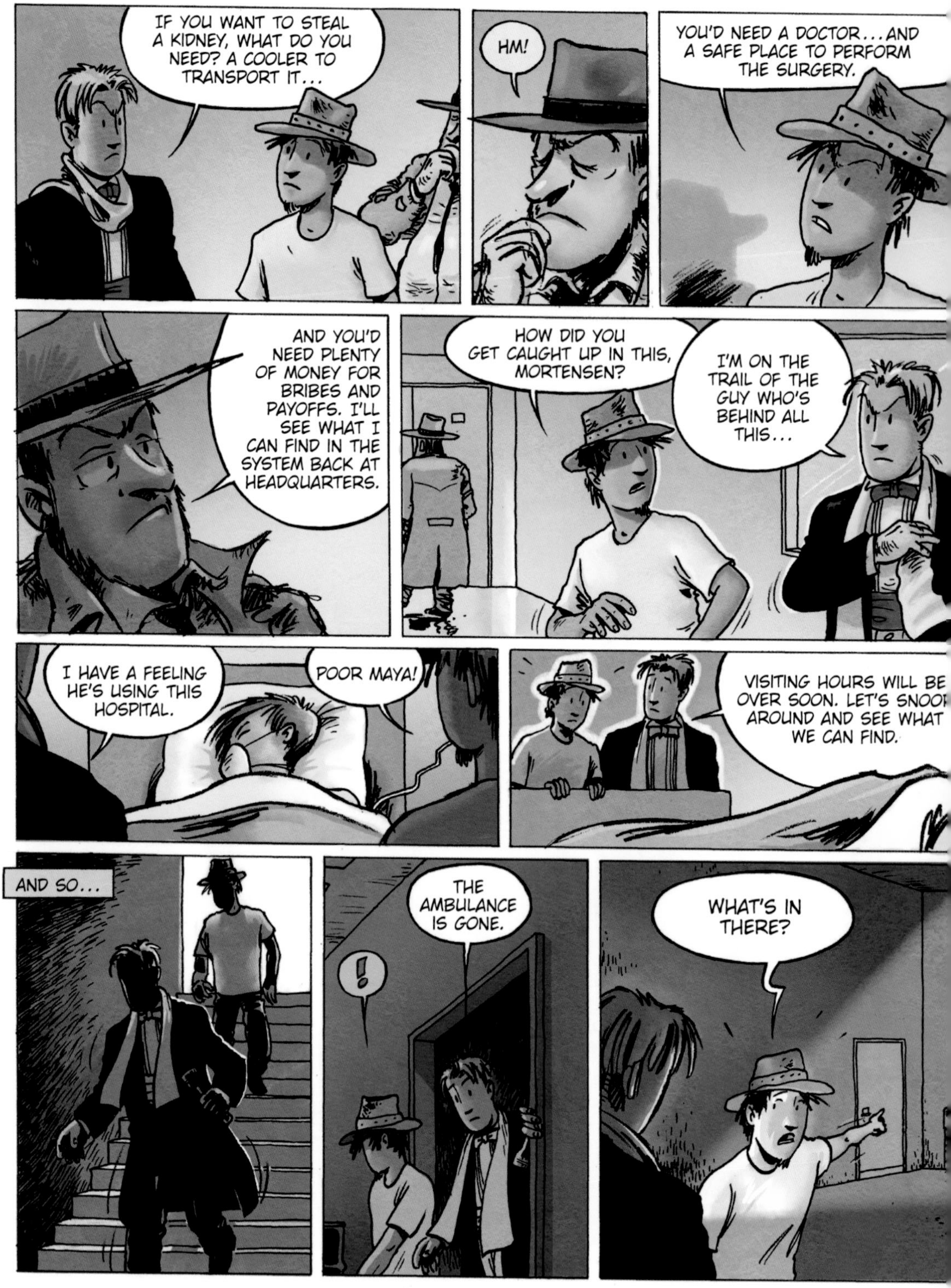
IF YOU WANT TO STEAL A KIDNEY, WHAT DO YOU NEED? A COOLER TO TRANSPORT IT...
HM!
YOU'D NEED A DOCTOR...AND A SAFE PLACE TO PERFORM THE SURGERY.
AND YOU'D NEED PLENTY OF MONEY FOR BRIBES AND PAYOFFS. I'LL SEE WHAT I CAN FIND IN THE SYSTEM BACK AT HEADQUARTERS.
HOW DID YOU GET CAUGHT UP IN THIS, MORTENSEN?
I'M ON THE TRAIL OF THE GUY WHO'S BEHIND ALL THIS...
I HAVE A FEELING HE'S USING THIS HOSPITAL.
POOR MAYA!
VISITING HOURS WILL BE OVER SOON. LET'S SNOOP AROUND AND SEE WHAT WE CAN FIND.
AND SO...
!
THE AMBULANCE IS GONE.
WHAT'S IN THERE?

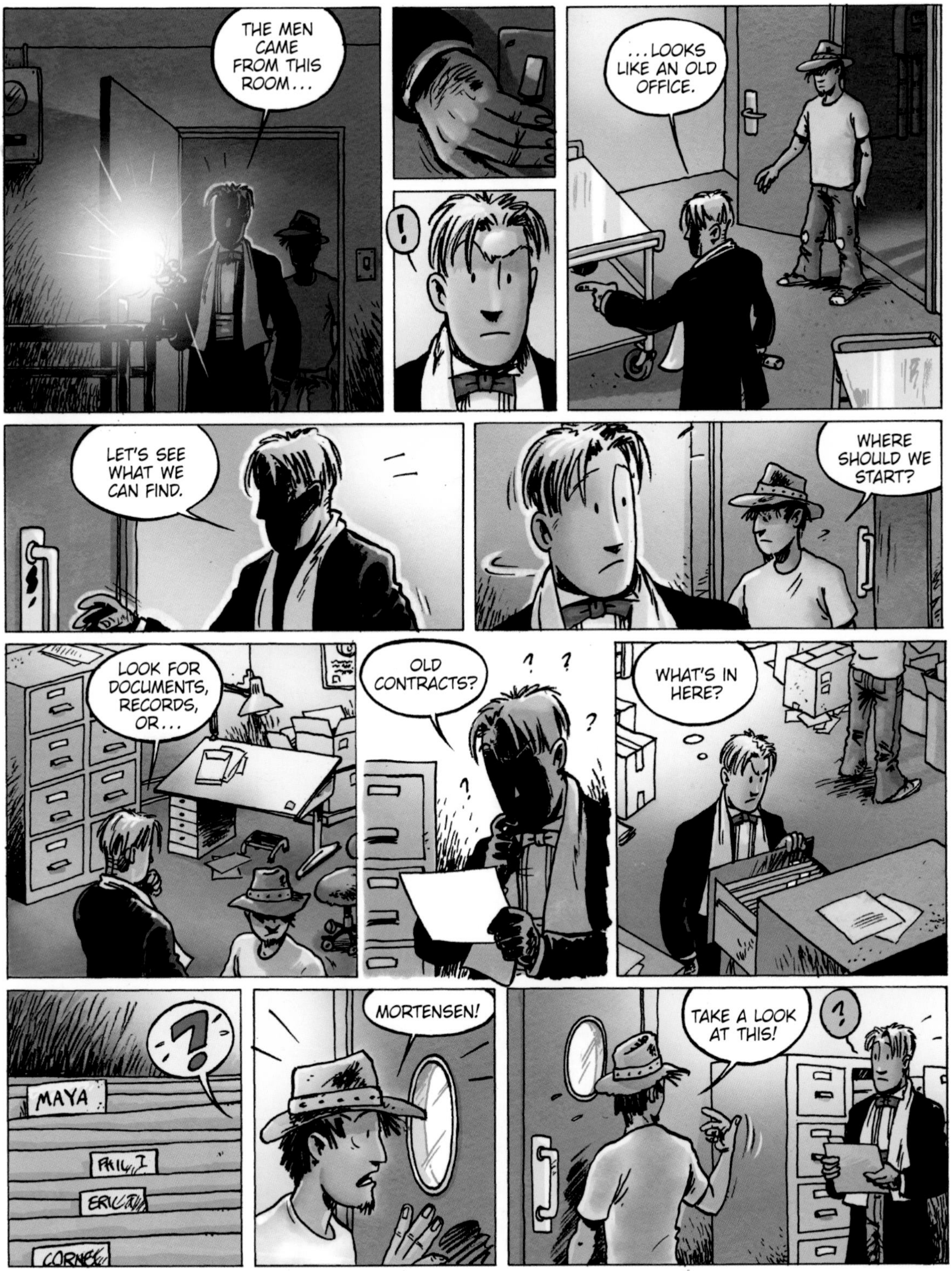
THE MEN CAME FROM THIS ROOM...
!
...LOOKS LIKE AN OLD OFFICE.
LET'S SEE WHAT WE CAN FIND.
WHERE SHOULD WE START?
LOOK FOR DOCUMENTS, RECORDS, OR...
OLD CONTRACTS?
? ? ? ?
WHAT'S IN HERE?
?
MAYA
ERIC
MORTENSEN!
TAKE A LOOK AT THIS!
?

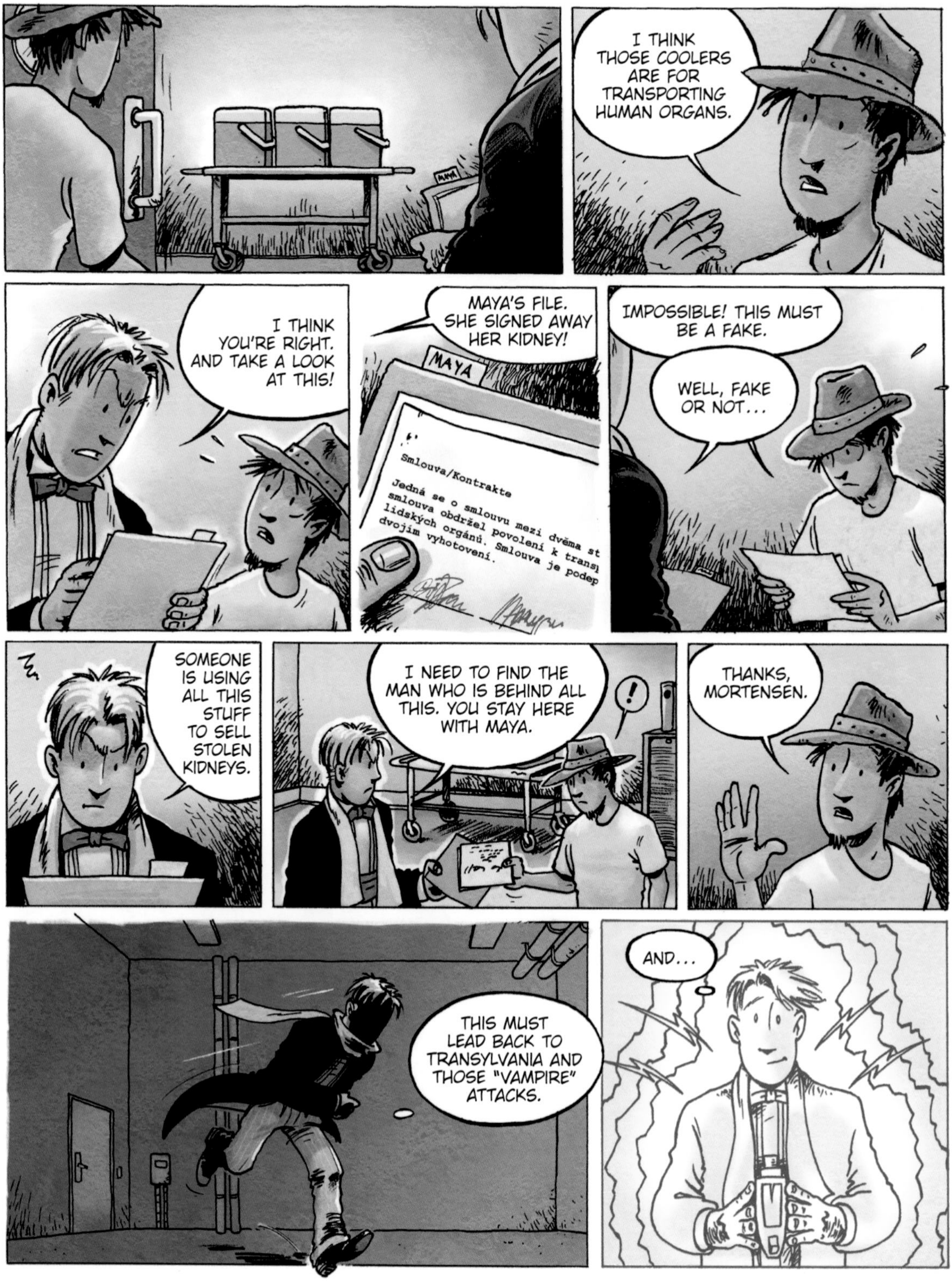
MAYA
I THINK THOSE COOLERS ARE FOR TRANSPORTING HUMAN ORGANS.
I THINK YOU'RE RIGHT. AND TAKE A LOOK AT THIS!
MAYA'S FILE. SHE SIGNED AWAY HER KIDNEY!
MAYA
Smlouva/Kontrakte
Jedná se o smlouvu mezi dvěma st
smlouva obdržel povolení k trans
lidských orgánů. Smlouva je podep
dvojím vyhotovení.
IMPOSSIBLE! THIS MUST BE A FAKE.
WELL, FAKE OR NOT...
SOMEONE IS USING ALL THIS STUFF TO SELL STOLEN KIDNEYS.
I NEED TO FIND THE MAN WHO IS BEHIND ALL THIS. YOU STAY HERE WITH MAYA.
!
THANKS, MORTENSEN.
THIS MUST LEAD BACK TO TRANSYLVANIA AND THOSE "VAMPIRE" ATTACKS.
AND...

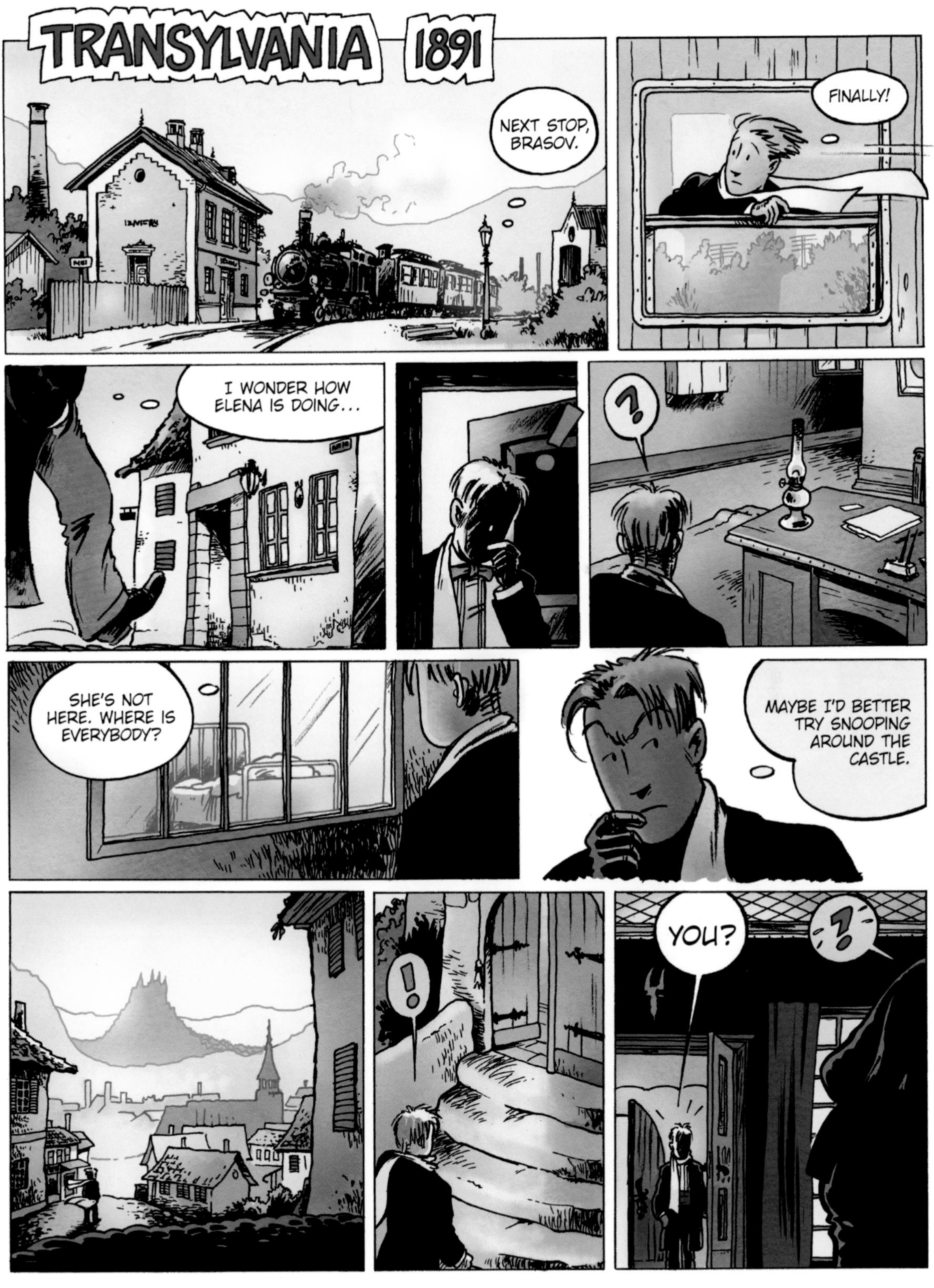
TRANSYLVANIA 1891
NEXT STOP, BRASOV.
FINALLY!
I WONDER HOW ELENA IS DOING...
?
SHE'S NOT HERE. WHERE IS EVERYBODY?
MAYBE I'D BETTER TRY SNOOPING AROUND THE CASTLE.
!
YOU?
?

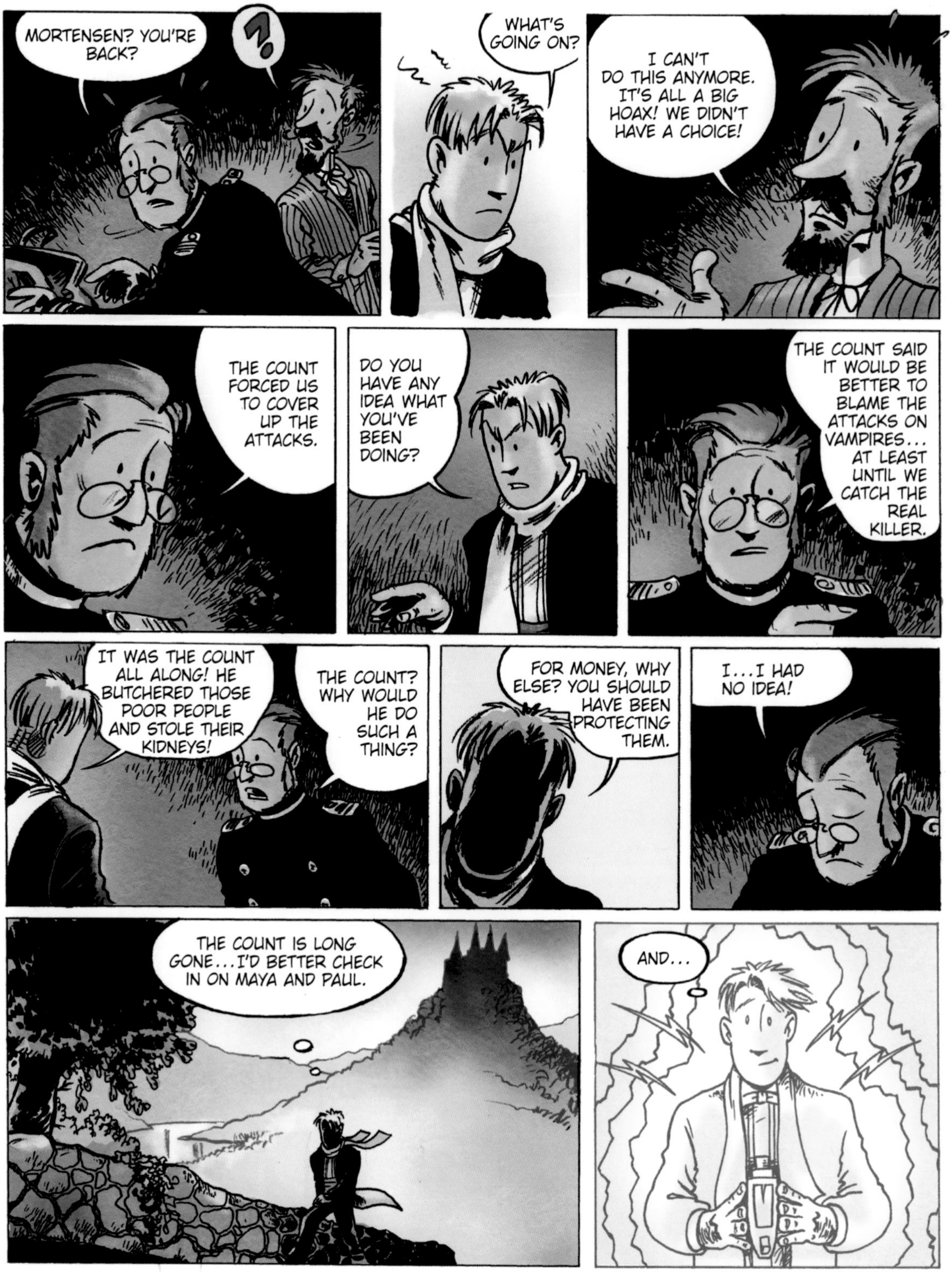
MORTENSEN? YOU'RE BACK?
?
WHAT'S GOING ON?
I CAN'T DO THIS ANYMORE. IT'S ALL A BIG HOAX! WE DIDN'T HAVE A CHOICE!
THE COUNT FORCED US TO COVER UP THE ATTACKS.
DO YOU HAVE ANY IDEA WHAT YOU'VE BEEN DOING?
THE COUNT SAID IT WOULD BE BETTER TO BLAME THE ATTACKS ON VAMPIRES... AT LEAST UNTIL WE CATCH THE REAL KILLER.
IT WAS THE COUNT ALL ALONG! HE BUTCHERED THOSE POOR PEOPLE AND STOLE THEIR KIDNEYS!
THE COUNT? WHY WOULD HE DO SUCH A THING?
FOR MONEY, WHY ELSE? YOU SHOULD HAVE BEEN PROTECTING THEM.
I...I HAD NO IDEA!
THE COUNT IS LONG GONE...I'D BETTER CHECK IN ON MAYA AND PAUL.
AND...

GOOD MORNING! HOW ARE YOU FEELING?

MORTENSEN! MAYA IS FEELING BETTER...

I STILL HAVEN'T CRACKED THIS CASE. WE MUST HAVE MISSED SOMETHING.

EVERYTHING IS QUIET AROUND HERE. I HAVEN'T SEEN THOSE STRANGE MEN AROUND.

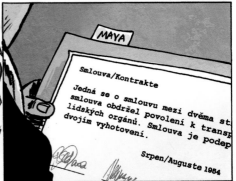

WERE YOU SNOOPING IN THAT OFFICE AGAIN?

I HAD TO GET MAYA'S CONTRACT! I KNEW SOMETHING DIDN'T LOOK RIGHT.

LET'S SEE.

MAYA

Smlouva/Kontrakte

Jedná se o smlouvu mezi dvěma st
smlouva obdržel povolení k transp
lidských orgánů. Smlouva je podep
dvojím vyhotovení.

Srpen/Auguste 1954

WELL, WHAT ABOUT IT?

DIDN'T YOU SEE? IT WAS SIGNED IN PARIS, IN 1954!

!

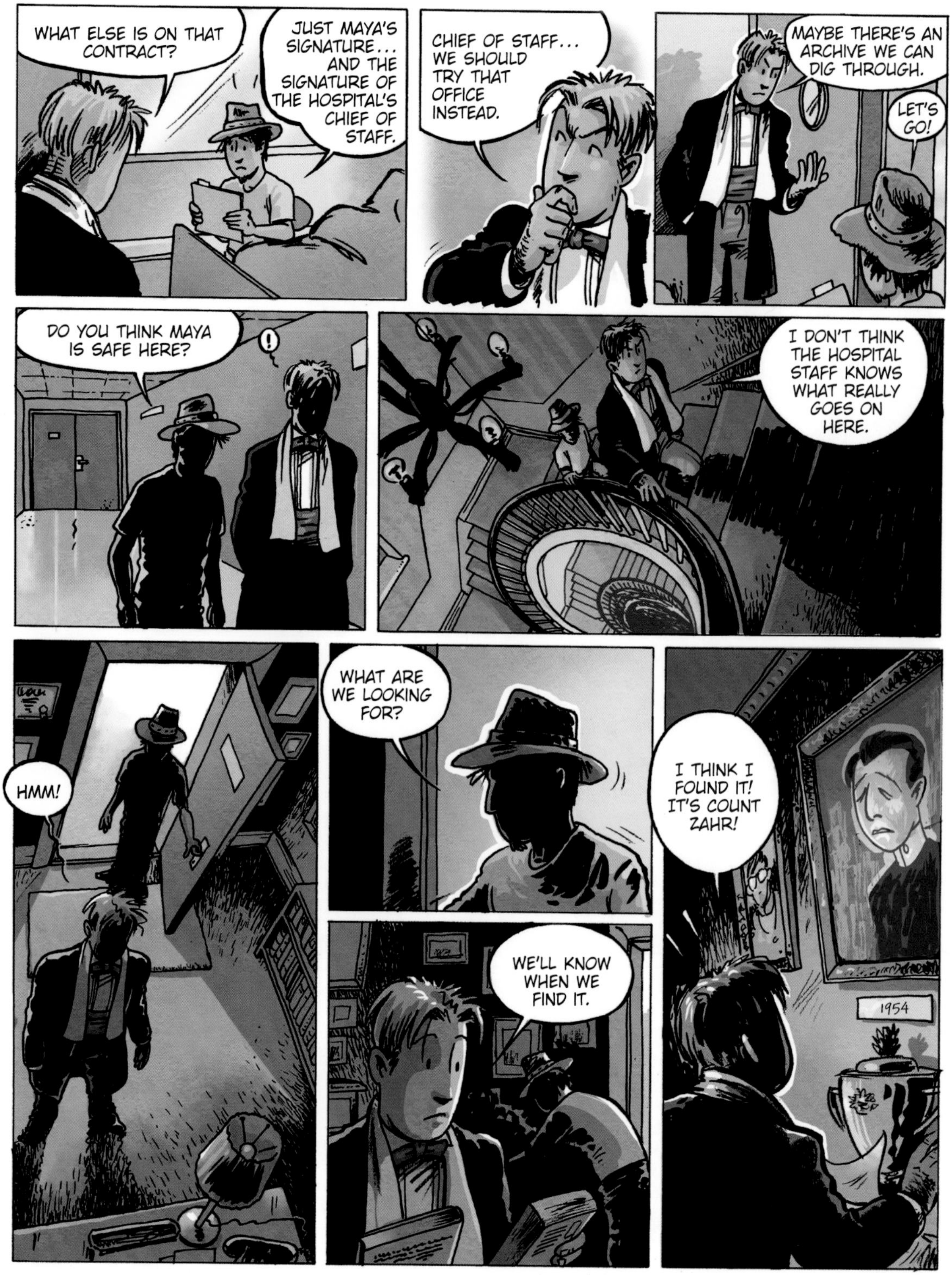

WHAT ELSE IS ON THAT CONTRACT?
JUST MAYA'S SIGNATURE... AND THE SIGNATURE OF THE HOSPITAL'S CHIEF OF STAFF.
CHIEF OF STAFF... WE SHOULD TRY THAT OFFICE INSTEAD.
MAYBE THERE'S AN ARCHIVE WE CAN DIG THROUGH.
LET'S GO!
DO YOU THINK MAYA IS SAFE HERE?
!
I DON'T THINK THE HOSPITAL STAFF KNOWS WHAT REALLY GOES ON HERE.
HMM!
WHAT ARE WE LOOKING FOR?
WE'LL KNOW WHEN WE FIND IT.
I THINK I FOUND IT! IT'S COUNT ZAHR!
1954

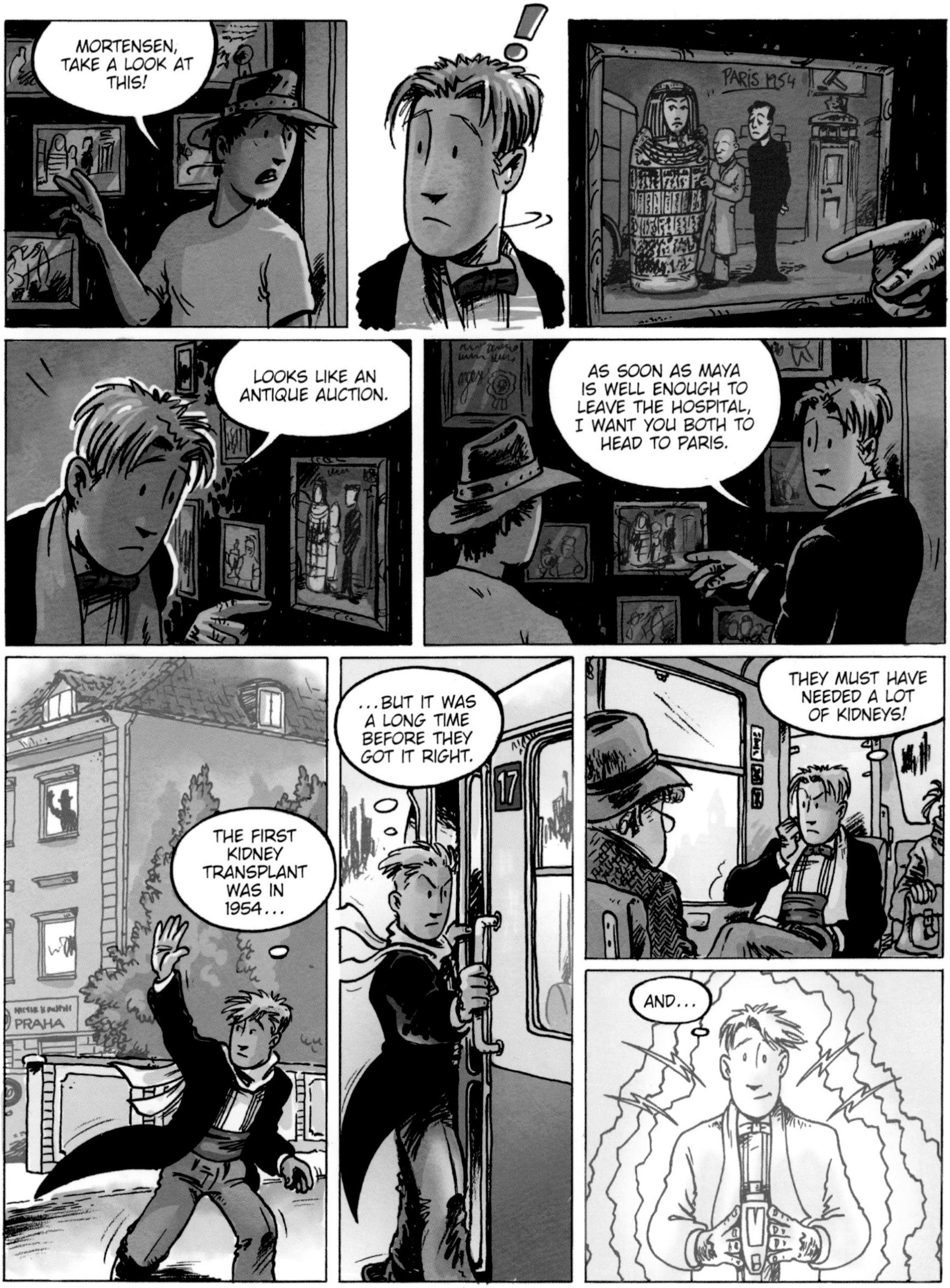
MORTENSEN, TAKE A LOOK AT THIS!
!
PARIS 1954
LOOKS LIKE AN ANTIQUE AUCTION.
AS SOON AS MAYA IS WELL ENOUGH TO LEAVE THE HOSPITAL, I WANT YOU BOTH TO HEAD TO PARIS.
PRAHA
THE FIRST KIDNEY TRANSPLANT WAS IN 1954...
...BUT IT WAS A LONG TIME BEFORE THEY GOT IT RIGHT.
17
THEY MUST HAVE NEEDED A LOT OF KIDNEYS!
AND...

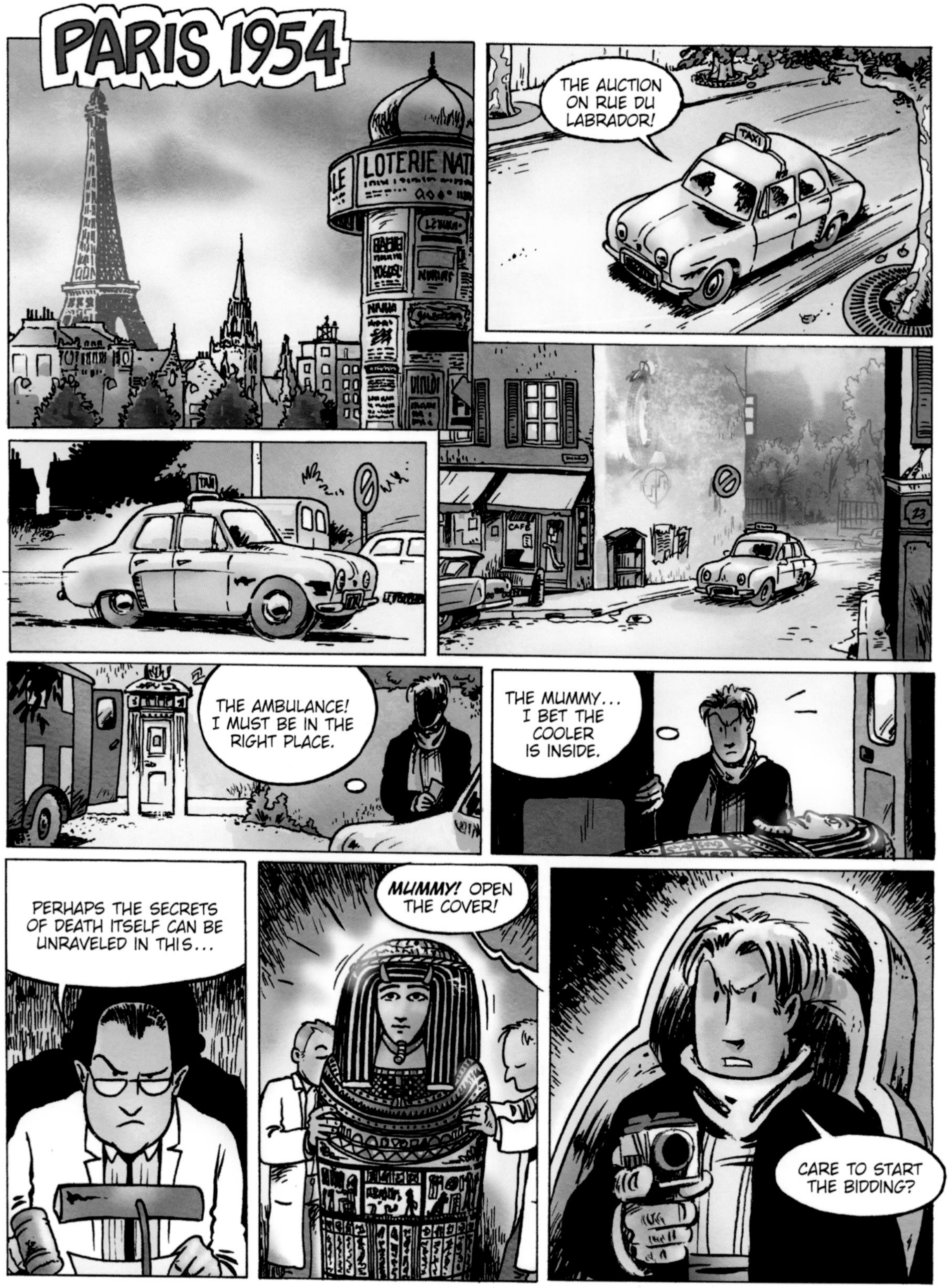
PARIS 1954
LOTERIE NAT
THE AUCTION ON RUE DU LABRADOR!
TAXI
THE AMBULANCE! I MUST BE IN THE RIGHT PLACE.
THE MUMMY... I BET THE COOLER IS INSIDE.
PERHAPS THE SECRETS OF DEATH ITSELF CAN BE UNRAVELED IN THIS...
MUMMY! OPEN THE COVER!
CARE TO START THE BIDDING?

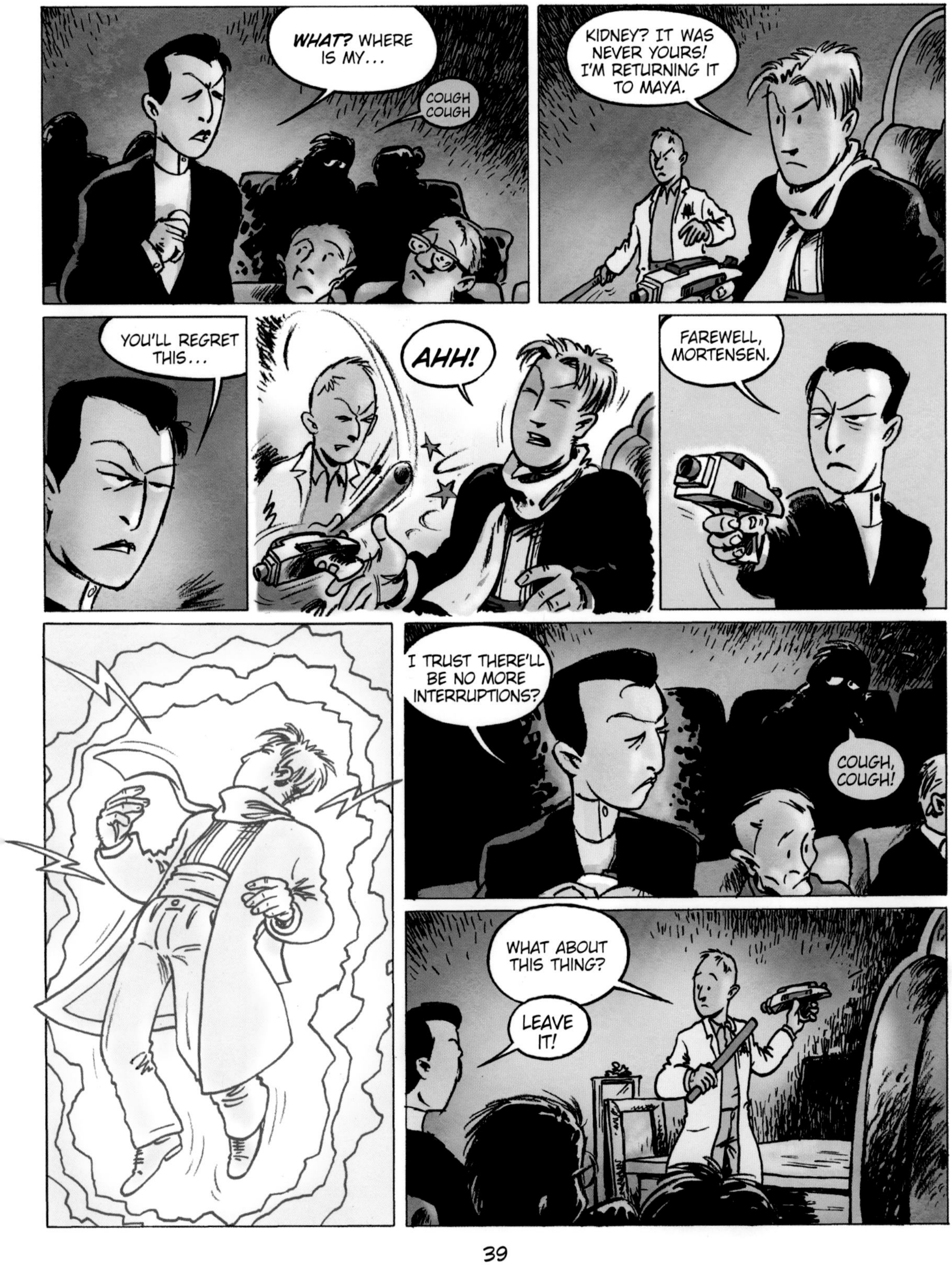

WHAT? WHERE IS MY...
COUGH COUGH
KIDNEY? IT WAS NEVER YOURS! I'M RETURNING IT TO MAYA.
YOU'LL REGRET THIS...
AHH!
FAREWELL, MORTENSEN.
I TRUST THERE'LL BE NO MORE INTERRUPTIONS?
COUGH, COUGH!
WHAT ABOUT THIS THING?
LEAVE IT!

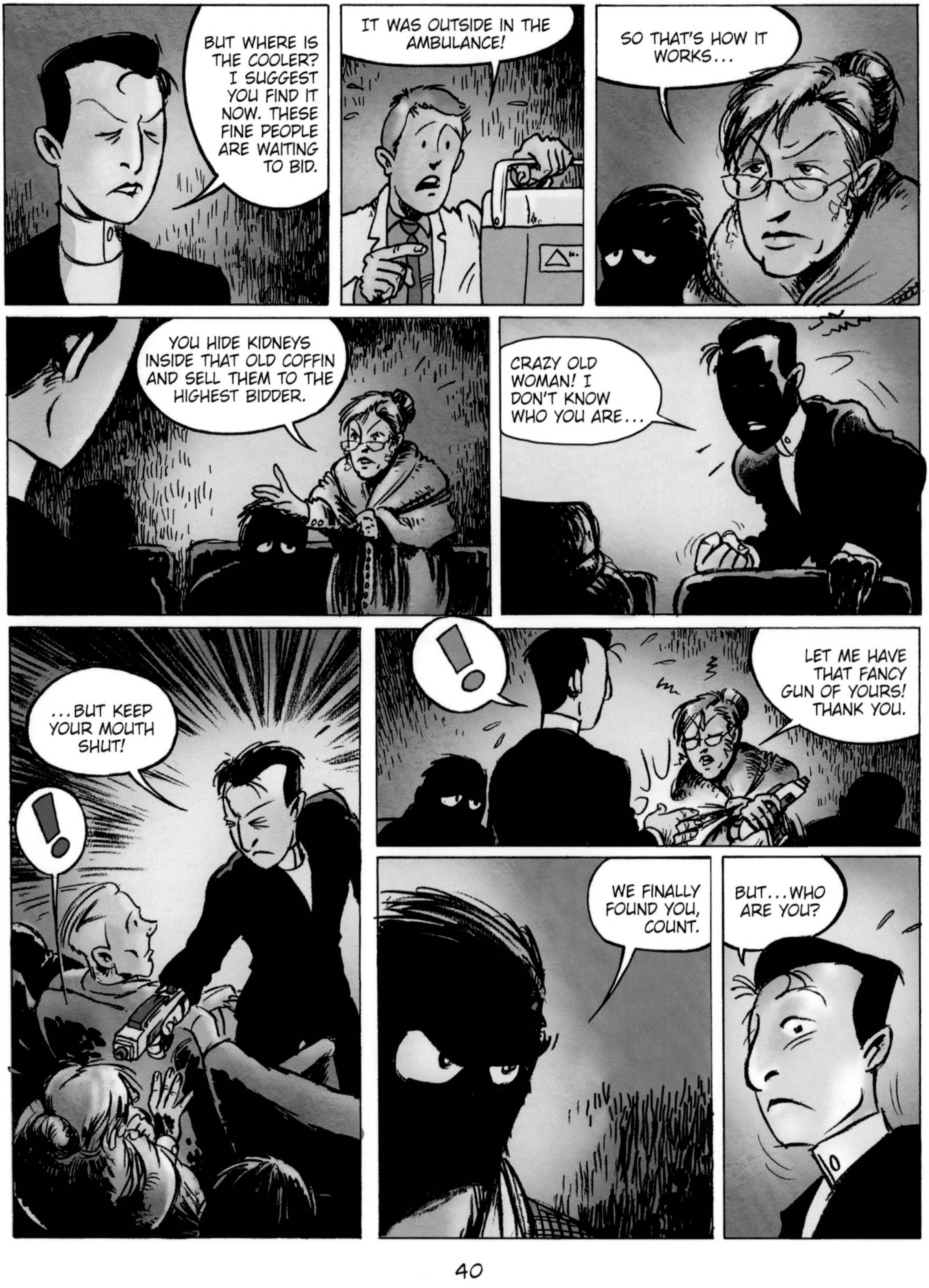

BUT WHERE IS THE COOLER? I SUGGEST YOU FIND IT NOW. THESE FINE PEOPLE ARE WAITING TO BID.
IT WAS OUTSIDE IN THE AMBULANCE!
SO THAT'S HOW IT WORKS...
YOU HIDE KIDNEYS INSIDE THAT OLD COFFIN AND SELL THEM TO THE HIGHEST BIDDER.
CRAZY OLD WOMAN! I DON'T KNOW WHO YOU ARE...
...BUT KEEP YOUR MOUTH SHUT!
!
!
LET ME HAVE THAT FANCY GUN OF YOURS! THANK YOU.
WE FINALLY FOUND YOU, COUNT.
BUT...WHO ARE YOU?

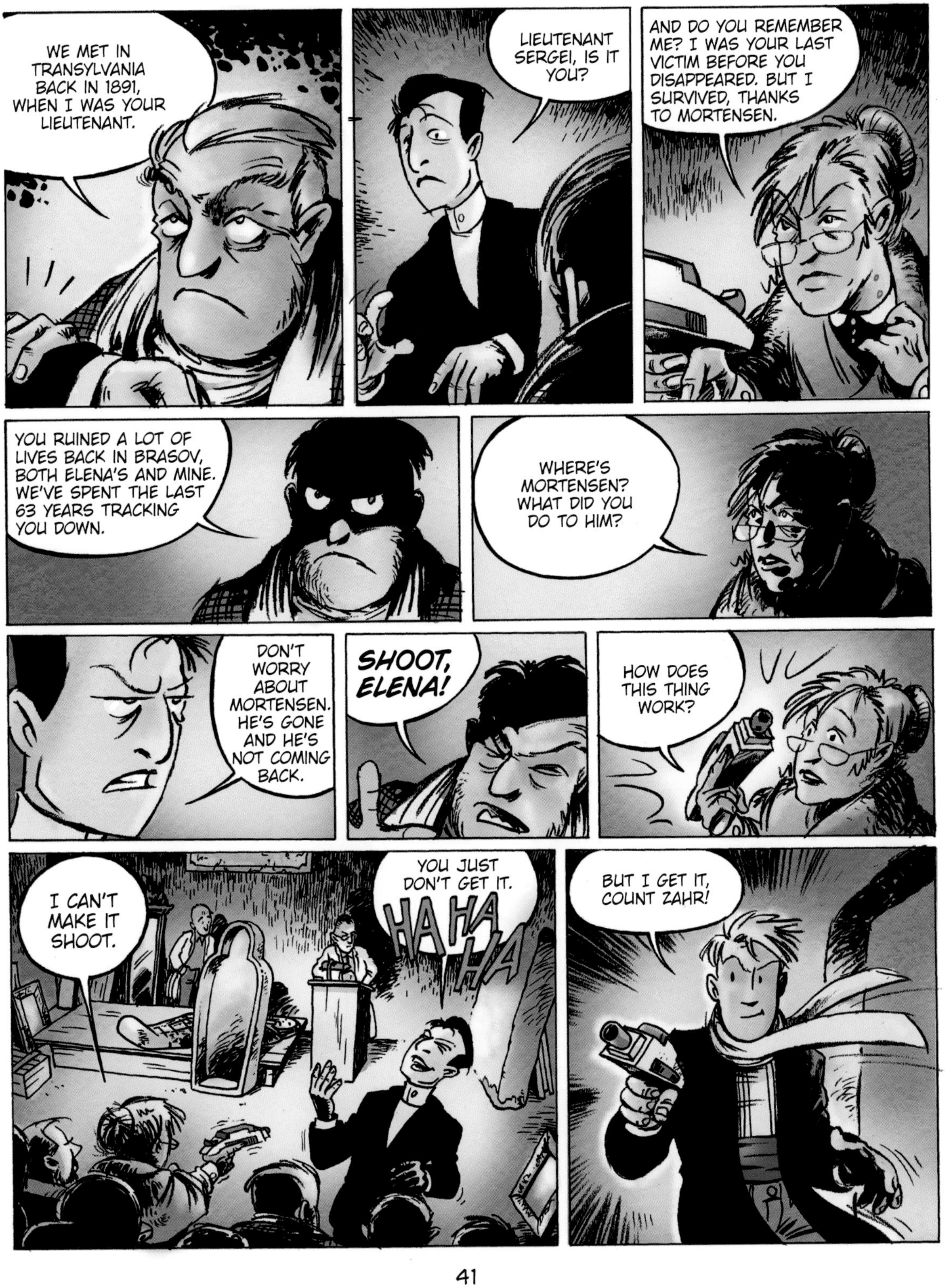
WE MET IN TRANSYLVANIA BACK IN 1891, WHEN I WAS YOUR LIEUTENANT.
LIEUTENANT SERGEI, IS IT YOU?
AND DO YOU REMEMBER ME? I WAS YOUR LAST VICTIM BEFORE YOU DISAPPEARED. BUT I SURVIVED, THANKS TO MORTENSEN.
YOU RUINED A LOT OF LIVES BACK IN BRASOV, BOTH ELENA'S AND MINE. WE'VE SPENT THE LAST 63 YEARS TRACKING YOU DOWN.
WHERE'S MORTENSEN? WHAT DID YOU DO TO HIM?
DON'T WORRY ABOUT MORTENSEN. HE'S GONE AND HE'S NOT COMING BACK.
SHOOT, ELENA!
HOW DOES THIS THING WORK?
I CAN'T MAKE IT SHOOT.
YOU JUST DON'T GET IT.
HAHAHA
BUT I GET IT, COUNT ZAHR!

MORTENSEN? BUT HOW?

DON'T MOVE, COUNT ZAHR. THE POLICE HAVE THIS PLACE SURROUNDED. THERE'S NOWHERE TO RUN.

WHAT? NO!

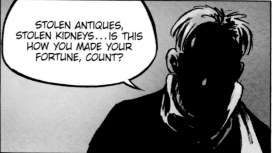

STOLEN ANTIQUES, STOLEN KIDNEYS...IS THIS HOW YOU MADE YOUR FORTUNE, COUNT?

GRAB HIM! HE'S GOT A TIME GUN!

A TIME GUN? YOU READ TOO MANY COMIC BOOKS!

I TOLD YOU, HE'S A COMPLETE NUTCASE!

WHERE DID YOU GET THE EXTRA TIME GUN?

I NABBED IT FROM YOUR AMBULANCE. NEVER HURTS TO HAVE A SPARE. IF YOU'LL EXCUSE ME, MAYA NEEDS THIS.

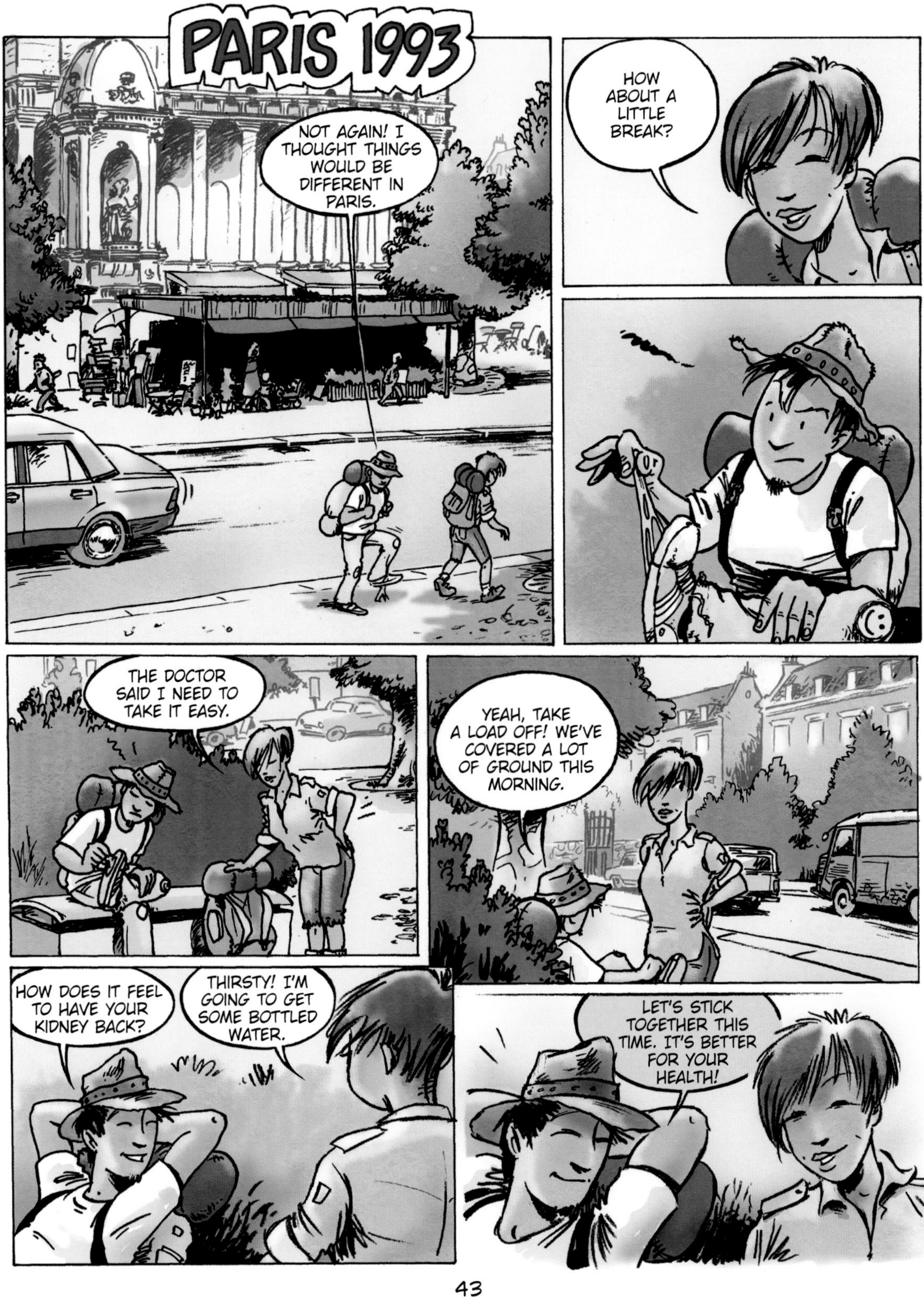
PARIS 1993
NOT AGAIN! I THOUGHT THINGS WOULD BE DIFFERENT IN PARIS.
HOW ABOUT A LITTLE BREAK?
THE DOCTOR SAID I NEED TO TAKE IT EASY.
YEAH, TAKE A LOAD OFF! WE'VE COVERED A LOT OF GROUND THIS MORNING.
HOW DOES IT FEEL TO HAVE YOUR KIDNEY BACK?
THIRSTY! I'M GOING TO GET SOME BOTTLED WATER.
LET'S STICK TOGETHER THIS TIME. IT'S BETTER FOR YOUR HEALTH!

The Real Dracula

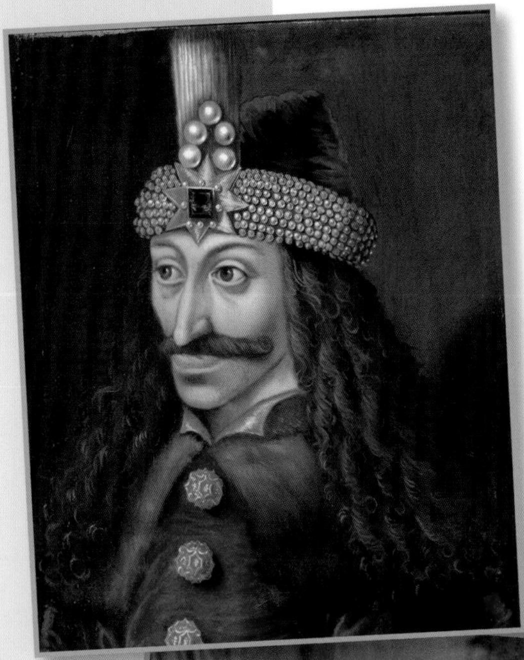

Though the villain in Bram Stoker's novel *Dracula* is a fictional character, he was inspired by a real person. Vlad III was a 15th-century prince in a region called Wallachia (located in modern-day Romania). His father, Vlad II, went by the nickname Dracul, or "the dragon." He got this nickname because he was a member of the Order of the Dragon, a society of Christian noblemen who fought against the Ottoman Empire.

Wallachia was a war-torn region. Both the Ottoman Empire and Hungary fought bitterly for its dominance. Dracul's sons were caught up in these political battles. As a child, Vlad III was held hostage by the Ottoman Empire. Later, his father and brother were viciously assassinated by Hungarian forces. This probably contributed to Vlad III's thirst for power and his hatred of Ottoman Turks.

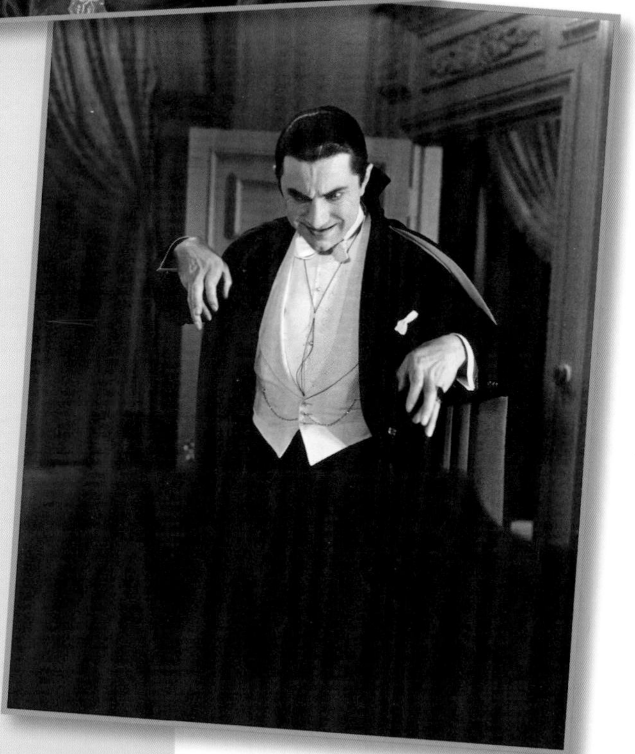

Vlad III sometimes signed his name Dracula, or "son of the Dragon." He was also known by another name—Vlad Tepes, which means "Vlad the Impaler." He got his nickname from his preferred method of executing political enemies. It is estimated that his victims number in the tens of thousands. Vlad III became infamous thanks in part to pamphlets and woodcuts that illustrated his misdeeds—making Dracula's story a best seller centuries before Bram Stoker wrote his novel.

Transylvania

Transylvania is a real place—it's a region of western Romania bordered by the Carpathian Mountains. Several different groups of people have laid claim to this territory, including the Celts, the Saxons, and the Roman Empire. Hungary took possession of it in the 11th century but lost it to the Ottoman Empire in the 16th century. While under Ottoman control, the region was largely independent. This independence, along with the area's turbulent history and Turkish influence, made it seem exotic and mysterious to a Victorian like Bram Stoker.

Bran Castle is located near Brasov, on the border between Transylvania and Wallachia. It was built along an important trade route that was also utilized by invading armies. Though Castle Bran is marketed as Castle Dracula, it seems Vlad III had little connection to it, nor was it the intended locale for Bram Stoker's novel.

Egyptian Sarcophagi

The ancient Egyptians believed that having a preserved, intact body after death was essential to reach the afterlife. They would remove the internal organs of the deceased and then dry out and preserve the rest of the body to prevent decomposition. After bodies were mummified, they were put in sarcophagi (coffins) to protect them from animals. Mummification was very expensive, so the poor would have sarcophagi made of reeds or clay. The rich pharaohs of Egypt would be buried in chambers intricately decorated and filled with treasure, with multiple coffins surrounding the body. The inner coffins were usually made of wood or metal, while the outermost was made of a single slab of carved stone. Most of the sarcophagi that exist today housed pharaohs. The most famous of these sarcophagi belonged to the pharaoh Tutankhamen (King Tut). Tut's solid gold inner sarcophagus is decorated with a pair of eyes so his spirit can see the burial offerings and has a false door so the spirit can escape.

The Kidney

The human body has two kidneys. They are located on each side of your body, near the lower back and right above your waist. These organs are about the size of a fist. Although they are small, kidneys are very important: they keep your blood clean. Things like digestion and the degeneration of old cells in the body produce waste. This waste is put into the blood, which is then sent to the kidneys. There, the waste is filtered out and sent to the bladder as urine, while the clean blood and nutrients the body needs are cycled back into the blood.

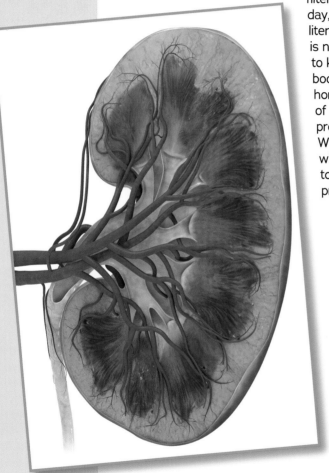

The kidneys are constantly working to keep your body clean. They filter 180 to 200 liters of blood every day, which produces only about 2 liters of urine. But cleaning the blood is not the kidneys' only job: they work to keep the amount of water in your body constant and they release hormones that stimulate the creation of red blood cells, regulate blood pressure, and help process calcium. Without functioning kidneys, waste will build up in the blood and the toxins will cause serious health problems and even death.

Kidney Transplantation

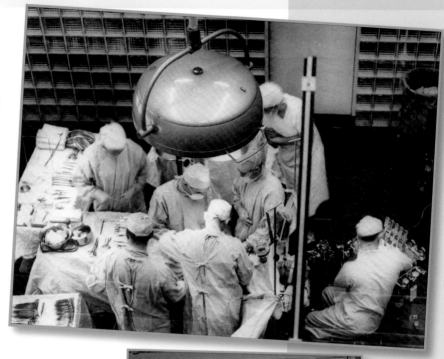

The idea of organ transplantation is an old one. One of the earliest known references states that in 500 B.C. a Chinese doctor swapped the hearts of two soldiers (according to legend, they lived to tell the tale). In truth, organ transplantation only became a reality in the 20th century. To save the lives of sick patients, surgeons tried to transplant human kidneys and also kidneys from animals such as monkeys and lambs. Initially, all these attempts were met with failure. The human immune system rejects and destroys foreign tissue and organs, so transplanted kidneys didn't last long. However, transplants between identical twins fare much better because they have body parts that are genetically similar. The first successful kidney transplant was performed in 1954 by Boston surgeon Joseph E. Murray. Richard Herrick received a kidney donated by his identical twin, Ronald.

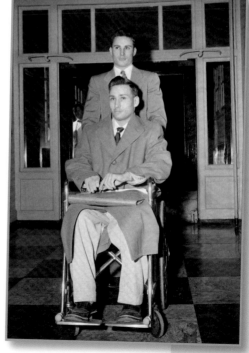

With modern advancements in tissue matching and immunosuppressive drugs, the success rate of kidney transplantation is much higher. Today, about 90 percent of the kidney transplants that come from living donors are successful.

The Bosnian War

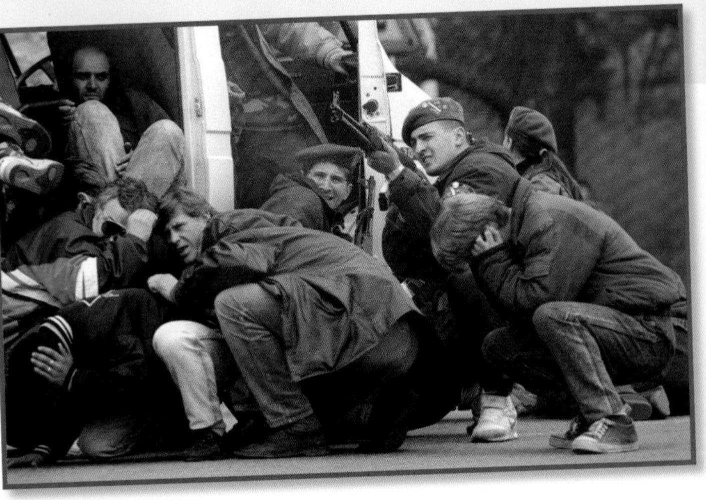

The Bosnian War (1992–1995) was fought in the country of Bosnia-Herzegovina. Bosnia was once part of the Socialist Federal Republic of Yugoslavia, but in the early 1990s, Yugoslavia broke into several countries, including Bosnia, Croatia, and Serbia. The leader of the newly formed Serbia was an ethnic nationalist and wanted to form a "pure" republic for a single ethnicity: the Serbs. Bosnia became a strong target for this genocidal ethnic cleansing, as it was the most ethnically diverse area. Serbia's army attacked Bosnian civilians, and the conflict turned neighbor against neighbor as people were forced to choose sides. The amount of death and destruction was terrible. After years of fighting, the war officially ended on December 14, 1995, with the signing of the Dayton Peace Accords. Though formally a single country, Bosnia was divided into two ethnically based sections. The Serbs gained control of the Republika Srpska, which comprises 49 percent of the country. The rest of the land was given to the Bosniaks and Croats, and it is called the Federation of Bosnia and Herzegovina.

The United Nations

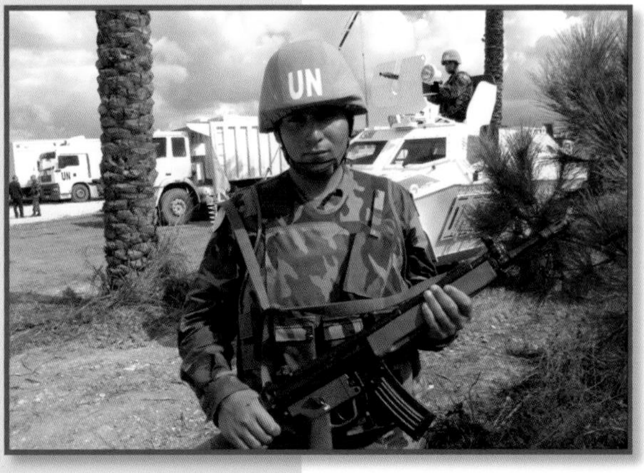
UN

The United Nations (UN) is an international organization that aims to promote cooperation and peace among countries and to help nations improve the lives of their current and future citizens by ending hunger, illiteracy, and disease. The United Nations was formed on October 24, 1945, modeled after the League of Nations, an international peacekeeping organization formed after the end of World War I (1914–1918). Unfortunately, the League didn't have its own military to carry out its decisions, and so it failed to stop World War II (1939–1945). After that war ended, 51 countries realized that they needed a stronger international governing organization to promote the League's original ideas of peace, as well as to address economic development and human rights. As of 2012 there were 193 member countries, and each gets a single vote. The decisions the UN makes are not binding, but they still carry weight because they are made by so many countries. It is up to the members of the UN to fund and see their resolutions through. There are many different organizations within the structure of the UN, and besides peacekeeping, they deal with issues such as disaster relief, gender equality, and terrorism.

Story and art by Lars Jakobsen
Translation by Lars Jakobsen and Robyn Chapman

First American edition published in 2013 by Graphic Universe™.
Copyright © 2012 by Lars Jakobsen
Translation copyright © 2013 by Lars Jakobsen
Graphic Universe™ is a trademark of Lerner Publishing Group, Inc.

Graphic Universe™
A division of Lerner Publishing Group, Inc.
241 First Avenue North
Minneapolis, MN 55401 U.S.A.

Website address: www.lernerbooks.com

Additional images in this book are used with the permission of: © Erich Lessing/Art Resource, NY, p. 44 (top); © Universal/The Kobal Collection/Art Resource, NY, p. 44 (bottom); © Warmcolors/Dreamstime.com, p. 45 (top); © Scott Olson/Getty Images, p. 45 (bottom); © Dorling Kindersley/Getty Images, p. 46; Brigham and Women's Hospital Archives, p. 47 (top); © Bettmann/CORBIS, p. 47 (bottom); © Mike Persson/AFP/Getty Images, p. 48 (top); © Sadikgulec/Dreamstime.com, p. 48 (bottom).

Main body text set in CC Wild Words 7.5/8.
Typeface provided by Comicraft/Active Images.

Library of Congress Cataloging-in-Publication Data

Jakobsen, Lars, 1964–
    [Falske mumie. English]
    The secret mummy / art by Lars Jakobsen ; story by Lars Jakobsen. — First American edition.
    pages cm. — (Mortensen's escapades ; #4)
    Originally published in Danish under title: Den falske mumie, in 2012.
    Summary: Mortimer Mortensen, a secret agent who travels through time to prevent thieves and saboteurs from rewriting history, uncovers a plot to steal human organs from living victims.
    ISBN: 978-0-7613-7915-7 (lib. bdg. : alk. paper)
    1. Graphic novels. [1. Graphic novels. 2. Time travel—Fiction. 3. Criminals—Fiction. 4. Transplantation of organs, tissues, etc.—Fiction.] I. Chapman, Robyn. II. Title.
PZ7.7.J648Se 2013
741.5'9489—dc23   2012027015

Manufactured in the United States of America
1 – BP – 12/31/12

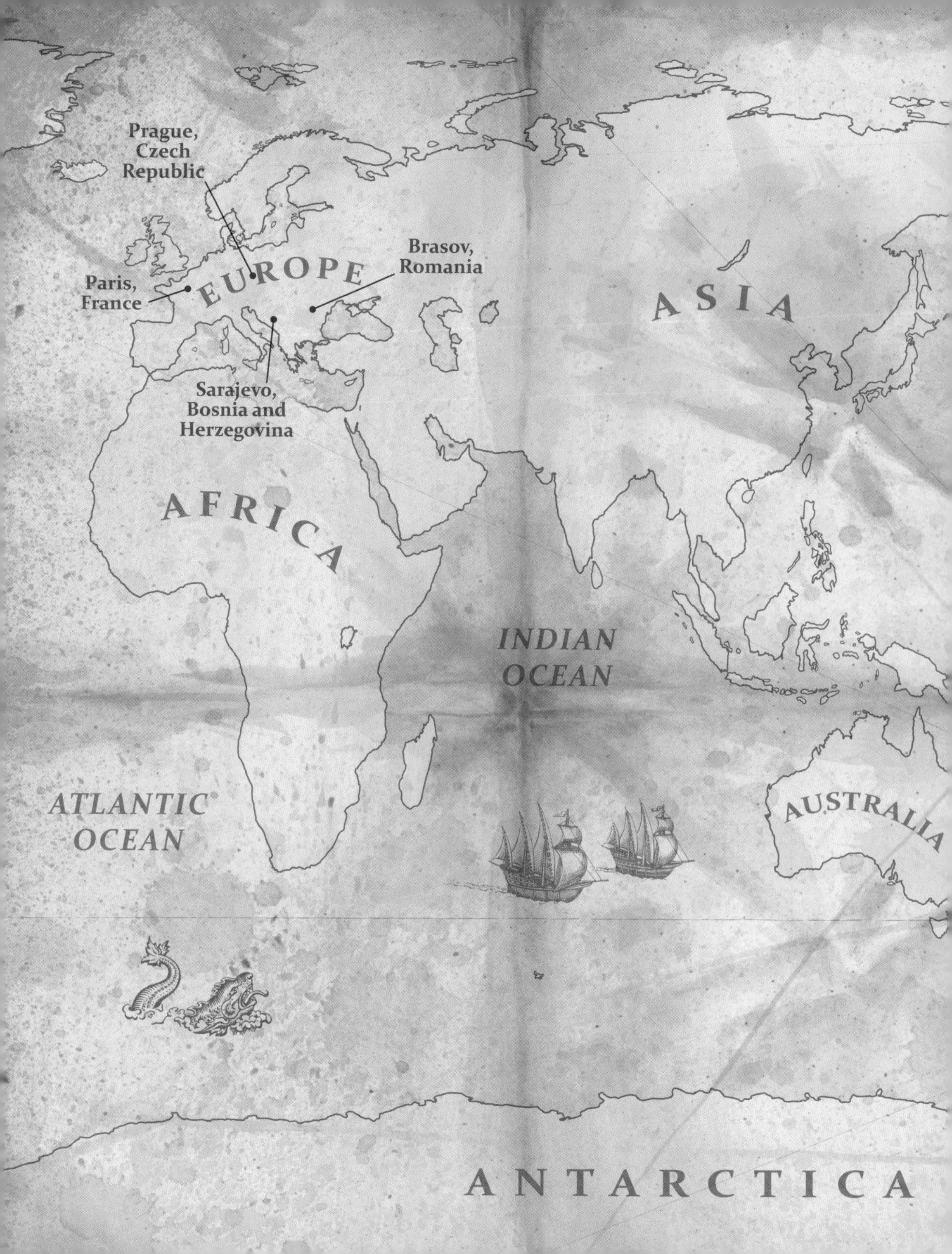
Prague,
Czech
Republic
Paris,
France
EUROPE
Brasov,
Romania
Sarajevo,
Bosnia and
Herzegovina
ASIA
AFRICA
INDIAN
OCEAN
ATLANTIC
OCEAN
AUSTRALIA
ANTARCTICA

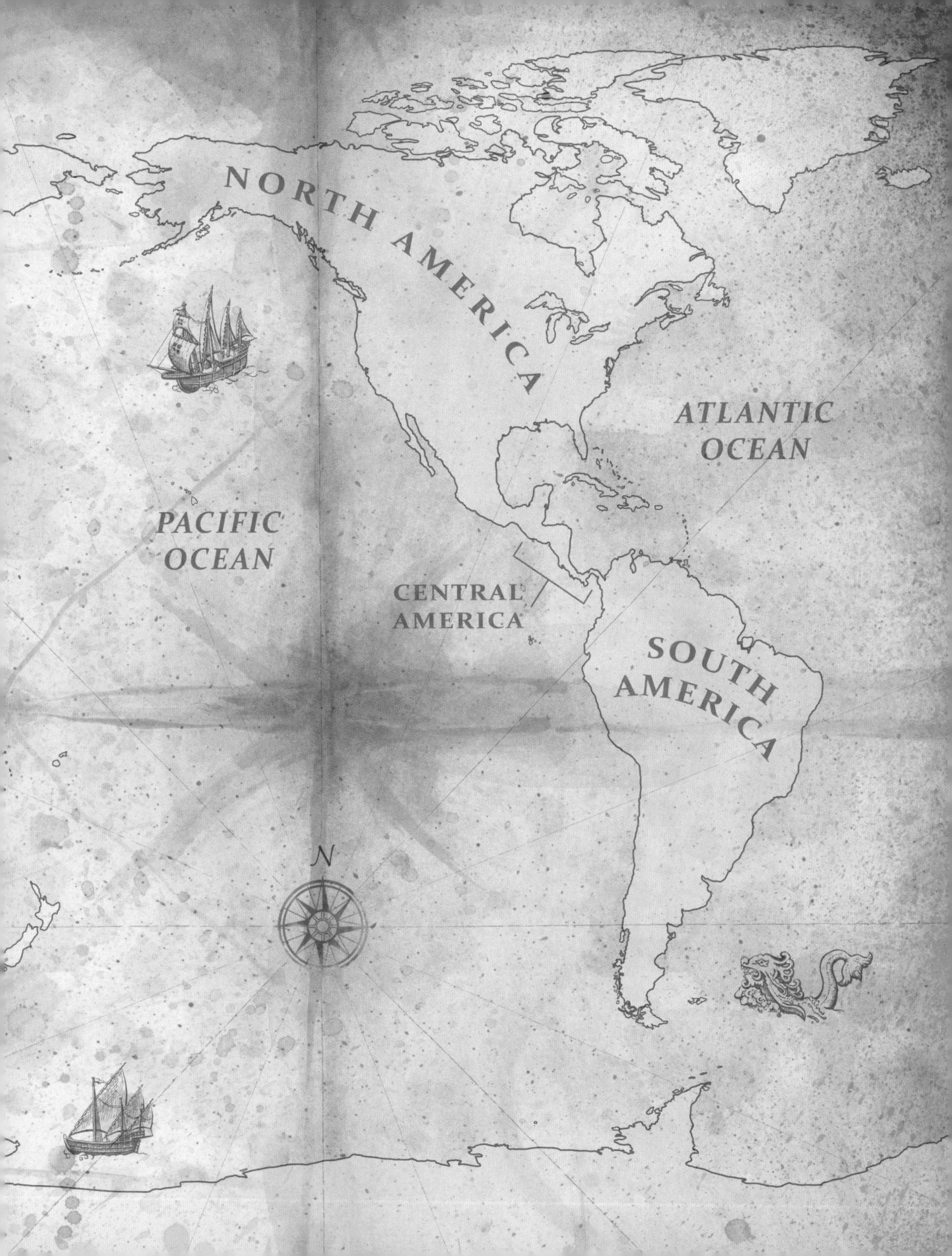
NORTH AMERICA
ATLANTIC OCEAN
PACIFIC OCEAN
CENTRAL AMERICA
SOUTH AMERICA
N